THE THING IN VAT 4

The sight that met my eyes was one of the most horrible I have ever looked upon. Something had evidently gone wrong with the culture medium, and instead of individual synthetic men being formed, there was a single huge mass of animal tissue emerging from the vat and rolling out over the floor. Human parts and organs grew out of it, a leg here, a hand there, a head somewhere else; and the heads were mouthing and screaming.

It would go on growing until it engulfed the building, the city . . . and perhaps all of Barsoom . . . unless it were destroyed.

And I knew of no way to destroy it.

Edgar Rice Burroughs
MARS NOVELS
Now available from Ballantine Books:

A PRINCESS OF MARS   (#1)

THE GODS OF MARS   (#2)

THE WARLORD OF MARS   (#3)

THUVIA, MAID OF MARS   (#4)

THE CHESSMEN OF MARS   (#5)

THE MASTER MIND OF MARS   (#6)

A FIGHTING MAN OF MARS   (#7)

SWORDS OF MARS   (#8)

SYNTHETIC MEN OF MARS   (#9)

LLANA OF GATHOL   (#10)

JOHN CARTER OF MARS   (#11)

SYNTHETIC MEN OF MARS

Edgar Rice Burroughs

A Del Rey Book

BALLANTINE BOOKS • NEW YORK

A Del Rey Book
Published by Ballantine Books

Synthetic Men of Mars was first published in *Argosy* Magazine as a six-part serial, January 7 through February 11, 1939.
Copyright © 1938, 1939 Edgar Rice Burroughs, Inc.

ISBN 0-345-27842-9

This authorized edition published by arrangement with
Edgar Rice Burroughs, Inc.

First U.S. Printing: June 1963
Twelfth U.S. Printing: June 1980

First Canadian Printing: August 1963
Second Canadian Printing: June 1979

Cover art by Michael Whelan, Copyright © 1979
Edgar Rice Burroughs, Inc.

CONTENTS

SYNTHETIC MEN OF MARS

CHAPTER I

WHERE IS RAS THAVAS?

FROM PHUNDAHL at their western extremity, east to Toonol, the Great Toonolian Marshes stretch across the dying planet for eighteen hundred earth miles like some unclean, venomous, Gargantuan reptile—an oozy marshland through which wind narrow watercourses connecting occasional bodies of open water, little lakes, the largest of which covers but a few acres. This monotony of marsh and jungle and water is occasionally broken by rocky islands, themselves usually clothed in jungle verdure, the skeletal remains of an ancient mountain range.

Little is known of the Great Toonolian Marshes in other portions of Barsoom, for this inhospitable region is peopled by fierce beasts and terrifying reptiles, by remnants of savage aboriginal tribes long isolated, and is guarded at either extremity by the unfriendly kingdoms of Phundahl and Toonol which discourage intercourse with other nations and are constantly warring upon one another.

Upon an island near Toonol, Ras Thavas, The Master Mind of Mars, had labored in his laboratory for nearly a thousand years until Vobis Kan, Jeddak of Toonol, turned against him and drove him from his island home and later repulsed a force of Phundahlian warriors led by Gor Hajus, the Assassin of Toonol, which had sought to recapture the island and restore Ras Thavas to his laboratory upon his promise to devote his skill and learning to the amelioration of human suffering rather than to prostitute them to the foul purposes of greed and sin.

Following the defeat of his little army, Ras Thavas had disappeared and been all but forgotten as are the dead, among which he was numbered by those who had known him; but there were some who could never forget him. There was Valla Dia, Princess of Duhor, whose brain he had transferred to the head of the hideous old Xaxa, Jeddara of Phundahl, that Xaxa might acquire the young and beautiful body of Valla Dia. There was Vad Varo, her husband, one time assistant to Ras Thavas, who had restored her brain to her own body—Vad Varo, who had been born Ulysses Paxton in the United States of America and presumably died in a shell hole in France; and there was John Carter, Prince of Helium, Warlord of Mars, whose imagination had been intrigued by the tales Vad Varo had told him of the marvelous skill of a world's greatest scientist and surgeon.

John Carter had not forgotten Ras Thavas, and when an emergency arose in which the skill of this greatest of surgeons was the sole remaining hope, he determined to seek him out and find him if he still lived. Dejah Thoris, his princess, had suffered an appalling injury in a collision between two swift airships; and had lain unconscious for many weeks, her back broken and twisted, until the greatest surgeons of all Helium had at last given up all hope. Their skill had been only sufficient to keep her alive; it could not mend her.

But how to find Ras Thavas? That was the question. And then he recalled that Vad Varo had been the assistant of the great surgeon. Perhaps, if the master could not be found, the skill of the pupil might be adequate. Then, too, of all men upon Barsoom, Vad Varo would be most likely to know the whereabouts of Ras Thavas. And so John Carter determined to go first to Duhor.

He selected from his fleet a small swift cruiser of a new type that had attained a speed of four hundred miles an hour—over twice the speed of the older types which he had first known and flown through the thin air of Mars. He would have gone alone, but Carthoris and Tara and Thuvia pleaded with him not to do so. At last he gave in and consented to take one of the officers of his personal troops, a young padwar named Vor Daj. To him we are indebted for this remarkable tale of strange adventure upon the planet Mars; to him and Jason Gridley whose discovery of the Gridley Wave has made it possible for me to receive this story over the special Gridley radio receiving set which Jason Gridley built out here in Tarzana, and to Ulysses Paxton who translated it into English and sent it across some forty million miles of space.

I shall give you the story as nearly as possible in the words of Vor Daj as is compatible with clarity. Certain

Martian words and idioms which are untranslatable, measures of time and of distance will be usually in my own words; and there are occasional interpolations of my own that I have not bothered to assume responsibility for, since their origin will be obvious to the reader. In addition to these, there must undoubtedly have been some editing on the part of Vad Varo.

So now to the strange tale as told by Vor Daj.

CHAPTER II

THE MISSION OF THE WARLORD

I AM VOR DAJ. I am a padwar in The Warlord's Guard. By the standards of Earthmen, for whom I understand I am writing this account of certain adventures, I should long since have been dead of old age; but here on Barsoom I am still a very young man. John Carter has told me that it is a matter worthy of general public interest if an Earthman lives a hundred years. The normal life expectancy of a Martian is a thousand years from the time that he breaks the shell of the egg in which he has incubated for five years and from which he emerges just short of physical maturity, a wild creature that must be tamed and trained as are the young of the lower orders which have been domesticated by man. And so much of that training is martial that it sometimes seems to me that I must have stepped from the egg fully equipped with the harness and weapons of a warrior. Let this, then, serve as my introduction. It is enough that you know my name and that I am a fighting man whose life is dedicated to the service of John Carter of Mars.

Naturally I felt highly honored when The Warlord chose me to accompany him upon his search for Ras Thavas, even though the assignment seemed of a prosaic nature of offering little more than an opportunity to be with The Warlord and to serve him and the incomparable Dejah Thoris, his princess. How little I foresaw what was in store for me!

It was John Carter's intention to fly first to Duhor, which lies some ten thousand five hundred haads, or about four thousand earth miles, northwest of the Twin Cities of Helium, where he expected to find Vad Varo, from whom he hoped to learn the whereabouts of Ras Thavas, who, with the possible exception of Vad Varo, was the only person in the world whose knowledge and skill might rescue Dejah Thoris from the grave, upon the brink of which she had lain for weeks, and restore her to health.

It was 8:25 (12:13 A.M. Earth Time) when our trim, swift flier rose from the landing stage on the roof of The Warlord's palace. Thuria and Cluros were speeding across a brilliant starlit sky casting constantly changing double shadows across the terrain beneath us that produced an illusion of myriad living things in constant, restless movement or a surging liquid world, eddying and boiling; quite different, John Carter told me, from a similar aspect above Earth, whose single satellite moves at a stately, decorous pace across the vault of heaven.

With our directional compass set for Duhor and our motor functioning in silent perfection there were no navigational problems to occupy our time. Barring some unforeseen emergency, the ship would fly in an air line to Duhor and stop above the city. Our sensitive altimeter was set to maintain an altitude of 300 ads (approximately 3000 feet), with a safety minimum of 50 ads. In other words, the ship would normally maintain an altitude of 300 ads above sea level, but in passing over mountainous country it was assured a clearance of not less than 50 ads (about 490 feet) by a delicate device that actuates the controls as the ship approaches any elevation of the land surface that is less than 50 ads beneath its keel. I think I may best describe this mechanism by asking you to imagine a self-focusing camera which may be set for any distance, beyond which it is always in focus. When it approaches an object within less distance than that for which it has been adjusted it automatically corrects the focus. It is this change that actuates the controls of the ship, causing it to rise until the fixed focus is again achieved. So sensitive is this instrument that it functions as accurately by starlight as by the brightest sunlight. Only in utter darkness would it fail to operate; but even this single limitation is overcome, on the rare occasions that the Martian sky is entirely overcast by clouds, through the medium of a small beam of light which is directed downward from the keel of the ship.

Secure in our belief in the infallibility of our directional compass, we relaxed our vigilance and dozed throughout the night. I have no excuses to offer, nor did John Carter upbraid me; for, as he was prompt to admit, the fault was

10

as much his as mine. As a matter of fact, he took all the blame, saying that the responsibility was wholly his.

It was not until well after sunrise that we discovered that something was radically wrong in either our position or our timing. The snow clad Artolian Hills which surround Duhor should have been plainly visible dead ahead, but they were not—just a vast expanse of dead sea bottom covered with ochre vegetation, and, in the distance, low hills.

We quickly took our position, only to find that we were some 4500 haads southeast of Duhor; or, more accurately, 150° W. Lon., from Exum, and 15° N. Lat. This placed us about 2600 haads southwest of Phundahl, which is situated at the western extremity of The Great Toonolian Marshes.

John Carter was examining the directional compass. I knew how bitterly disappointed he must be because of the delay. Another might have railed at fate; but he only said, "The needle is slightly bent—just enough to carry us off our course. But perhaps it's just as well—the Phundahlians are far more likely to know where Ras Thavas is than anyone in Duhor. I thought of Duhor first, naturally, because we'd be sure of friendly aid there."

"That's more than we can expect in Phundahl, from what I've heard of them."

He nodded. "Nevertheless, we'll go to Phundahl. Dar Tarus, the jeddak, is friendly to Vad Varo; and so may be friendly to Vad Varo's friend. Just to be on the safe side, though, we'll go into the city as panthans."

"They'll think we're flying high," I said, smiling: "—two panthans in a ship of the princely house of The Warlord of Barsoom!"

A panthan is a wandering soldier of fortune, selling his services and his sword to whomever will pay him; and the pay is usually low, for everyone knows that a panthan would rather fight than eat; so they don't pay him very much; and what they do pay him, he spends with prodigality, so that he is quite broke again in short order.

"They won't see the ship," replied John Carter. "We'll find a place to hide it before we get there. You will walk to the gates of Phundahl in plain harness, Vor Daj." He smiled. "I know how well the officers of my ships like to walk."

As we flew on toward Phundahl we removed the insignia and ornaments from our harnesses that we might come to the gates in the plain leather of unattached panthans. Even

11

then, we knew, we might not be admitted to the city, as Martians are always suspicious of strangers and because spies sometimes come in the guise of panthans. With my assistance, John Carter stained the light skin of his body with the reddish copper pigment that he always carries with him against any emergency that requires him to hide his identity and play the role of a native red man of Barsoom.

Sighting Phundahl in the distance, we flew low, just skimming the ground, taking advantage of the hills to hide us from sentries on the city wall; and within a few miles of our destination The Warlord brought the flier to a landing in a little canyon beside a small grove of sompus trees into which we taxied. Removing the control levers, we buried them a short distance from the ship, blazing four surrounding trees in such a manner that we might easily locate the cache when we should return to the ship—if we ever did. Then we set out on foot for Phundahl.

CHAPTER III

THE INVINCIBLE WARRIORS

SHORTLY AFTER THE Virginian soldier of fortune had arrived on Mars he had been given the name Dotar Sojat by the green Martian Tharks into whose hands he had fallen; but with the lapse of years the name had been practically forgotten, as it had been used for only a brief period by a few members of that wild horde. The Warlord now decided to adopt it for this adventure, while I retained my own name which was quite unknown in this part of the world; and so it was that Dotar Sojat and Vor Daj, two wandering panthans, trudged through the low hills to the west of Phundahl on this still Barsoomian morning. The mosslike ochre vegetation gave forth no sound beneath our sandalled feet. We moved as silently as our hard, sharp shadows which dogged our footsteps toward the east. Gay plumed voiceless birds watched us from the branches of skeel and sorapus trees, as silent as the beautiful insects which hovered around the gorgeous blooms of the pimalia and gloresta which grew in profusion in every depression of the hills that held Barsoom's scant moisture longest. Mars is a world of vast silences where even voiced creatures are muted as though by the consciousness of impending death, for Mars is a dying world. We abhor noise; and so our voices, like our music, are soft and low; and we are a people of few words. John Carter has told me of the din of Earthly cities and of the brasses and the drums and the cymbals of Earthly music, of the constant, senseless chatter of millions of voices saying nothing. I believe that such as these would drive Martians insane.

We were still in the hills and not yet in sight of the city when our attention was attracted by sounds above and behind us. We turned simultaneously to look back, and the sight that met our eyes was so astonishing that we could scarcely believe the evidence of our own senses. About twenty birds were winging toward us. That in itself was sufficiently astonishing, since they were easily identifiable as malagors, a species long presumed to be extinct; but to add to the incredibility of the sight that met our eyes, a warrior bestrode each of the giant birds. It was quite evident that they must have seen us; so it was quite useless to attempt to hide from them. They were already dropping lower, and presently they were circling us. With this opportunity for closer observation I was impressed by a certain grotesquerie in the appearance of the warriors. There was something a little inhuman about them, and yet they were quite evidently human beings similar to ourselves. One of them carried a woman in front of him on the neck of the great bird that was his mount; but as they were all in constant motion I was unable to obtain a really good look at her; nor, by the same token, of the others.

Presently the twenty malagors alighted in a circle about us, and five of the warriors dismounted and approached us. Now it was that I saw what lent them their strange and unnatural appearance. They seemed the faulty efforts of a poor draftsman, come to life—animated caricatures of man. There was no symmetry of design about them. The left arm of one was scarce a foot long, while his right arm was so long that the hand dragged along the ground as he walked. Four-fifths of the face of one was above the eyes, while another had an equal proportion below the eyes. Eyes, noses, and mouths were usually misplaced; and were either too large or too small to harmonize with contiguous features. But there was one exception—a warrior who now dismounted and followed behind the five who were approaching us. He was a handsome, well formed man, whose trappings and weapons were of excellent quality and design—the serviceable equipment of a fighting man. His harness bore the in-

13

signia of a dwar, a rank comparable to that of captain in your Earthly military organizations. At a command from him, the five halted before reaching us; and he addressed us.

"You are Phundahlians?" he asked.

"We are from Helium," John Carter replied. "Our latest employment was there. We are panthans."

"You are my prisoners. Throw down your arms."

The faintest of smiles touched the lips of The Warlord. "Come and take them," he said. It was a challenge.

The other shrugged. "As you will. We outnumber you ten to one. We shall take you, but we may kill you in the taking. I advise you to surrender."

"And you will be wise if you let us go our way, for we have no quarrel with you; and if you pick one, we shall not die alone."

The dwar smiled an inscrutable smile. "As you will," he replied; and then he turned to the five and said, "Take them!" But as they advanced upon us, he did not come with them, but remained behind, quite contrary to the ethics which determine the behavior of Martian officers. He should have led them, engaging us himself and setting an example of courage to his men.

We whipped our longswords from their scabbards and met the five horrific creatures, standing back to back as they circled us. The blade of The Warlord wove a net of razor edged steel before him, while I did the best that I could to defend my prince and uphold the honor of my metal; and I did well, for I am accounted a great swordsman by John Carter himself, the greatest of all. Our antagonists were no match for us. They could not pierce our guards, even though they fought with an entire disregard of life, throwing themselves upon our blades and coming in again for further punishment. And that was the disheartening feature of the horrid encounter. Time and again I would run a fellow through, only to have him back away until my blade was out of his body and then come at me again. They seemed to suffer neither from shock nor pain and to know no fear. My blade severed the arm of one of them at the shoulder; and while another engaged me, the fellow stooped and recovered his sword with his other hand and tossed his severed arm to one side. John Carter decapitated one of his antagonists; but the body ran around cutting and slashing in apparent ungovernable fury until the dwar ordered several of his other warriors to capture and disarm it, and all the while the head lay gibbering and grimacing in the dust.

14

This was the first of our antagonists to be rendered permanently *hors de combat,* and suggested the only way that we might be victorious.

"Behead them, Vor Daj!" The Warlord directed, and even as he spoke he lopped the head from another.

I tell you, it was a gruesome sight. The thing kept on fighting, and its head lay on the ground screaming and cursing. John Carter had to disarm it, and then it lunged forward and struck him with the weight of its headless torso just below the knees, throwing him off balance. It was fortunate that I happened to see what was going on, for another of the creatures would have run The Warlord through had I not. I was just in time, and I caught the thing with a clean cut that sent its head toppling to the ground. That left only two of our antagonists, and these the dwar called off.

They withdrew to their mounts, and I saw that the officer was issuing instructions; but what he was saying, I could not overhear. I thought they would give up then and go away, for several of them rose from the ground on their great malagors; but the dwar did not even remount. He just stood there watching. Those who had taken to the air circled just above us, out of reach of our swords; and a number of their fellows dismounted and approached us; but they, too, kept their distance. The three severed heads lay upon the ground, reviling us. The bodies of two of them had been disarmed and trussed up, while that of the third dashed hither and thither pursued by a couple of its fellows who sought to entangle it in nets which they cast at it whenever they could come near enough to it.

These side lights I caught in swift glances, for my attention was more concerned with the action of those who soared above us, in an effort to determine what their next mode of attack would be; nor did I have long to wait before my curiosity was satisfied. Unslinging nets which they wore wrapped about their waists and which I had previously thought were only articles of apparel, they dragged them around and over us in an attempt to entangle us. With a growing sense of futility we slashed at the fabric; and though we cut it in places, we could not escape it; and when they dexterously dropped a couple of them over us we were hopelessly enmeshed. Then those who had surrounded us on foot rushed in and bound us. We fought, but even the great strength of The Warlord was of no avail against the entangling meshes of the nets and the brute strength of the hideous creatures who so greatly outnumbered him. I thought that they would probably kill us now, but at a word of command from their dwar, they fell back. Those in the air alighted and gathered up their nets. Several heads and arms were collected and tied to the backs of malagors, as were the headless bodies; and while these things were being attended to, the officer approached and talked with us. He seemed to bear us no ill will for the damage we had inflicted upon his warriors, and was gracious enough to compliment us upon our courage and swordsmanship.

"However," he added, "you would have been wise to have taken my advice and surrendered in the first place. It is a miracle that you were not killed or at least badly wounded. Only your miraculous swordsmanship saved you."

"The only miracle involved," replied John Carter, "is that any of your men escaped with their heads. Their swordsmanship is abominable."

The dwar smiled. "I quite agree with you, but what they lack in technique they more than make up for in brute strength and fearlessness and the fact that they must be dismembered in order to be rendered harmless. As you may have noticed, they can't be killed."

"And now that we are your prisoners," inquired The Warlord, "what do you intend doing with us?"

"I shall take you to my superiors. They will decide. What are your names?"

"This is Vor Daj. I am Dotar Sojat."

"You are from Helium, and you were going to Phundahl. Why?"

"As I have told you, we are panthans. We are looking for employment."

"You have friends in Phundahl?"

"None. We have never been there. If another city had been in our path, we should have offered our services there. You know how it is with panthans."

The man nodded. "Perhaps you will have fighting yet."

"Would you mind telling me," I asked, "what manner of creatures your warriors are? I have never seen men like them."

"Nor anyone else," he said. "They are called hormads. The less you see of them, the better you will like them. Now that you must admit that you are my prisoners, I have a suggestion to make. Bound as you are, the trip to Morbus will be most uncomfortable; and I do not wish to subject two such courageous fighting men to unnecessary discomfort. Assure me that you will not try to escape before we reach Morbus and I will remove your bonds."

It was evident that the dwar was quite a decent fellow. We accepted his offer gladly, and he removed our bonds himself; then he bade us mount behind a couple of his warriors. It was then that I first had a close view of the woman riding on one of the malagors in front of a hormad. Our eyes met, and I saw terror and helplessness mirrored in hers. I saw, too, that she was beautiful; then the great birds took off with a terrific flapping of giant wings, and we were on our way to Morbus.

CHAPTER IV

THE SECRET OF THE MARSHES

HANGING IN A NET on one side of the malagor upon which I was mounted was one of the heads we had struck off in our fight with the hormads. I wondered why they were preserving such a grisly trophy, and attributed it to some custom or superstition requiring the return of a body to its homeland for final disposal.

Our course lay south of Phundahl, which the leader was evidently seeking to avoid; and ahead I could see the vast Toonolian Marshes stretching away in the distance as far as the eye could see—a labyrinth of winding waterways threading desolate swampland from which rose occasional islands of solid ground, with here and there a darker area of forest and the blue of tiny lakes.

As I watched this panorama unfolding before us, I heard a voice suddenly exclaim, querulously, "Turn me over. I can't see a thing but the belly of this bird." It seemed to come from below me; and, glancing down, I saw that it was the head hanging in the net beneath me that was speaking. It lay in the net, facing upward toward the belly of the malagor, helpless to turn or to move itself. It was a gruesome sight, this dead thing speaking; and I must confess that it made me shudder.

"I can't turn you over," I said, "because I can't reach you; and what difference does it make anyway? What difference does it make whether your eyes are pointed in one direction or another? You are dead, and the dead cannot see."

17

"Could I talk if I were dead, you brainless idiot? I am not dead, because I cannot die. The life principle is inherent in me—in every tissue of me. Unless it be totally destroyed, as by fire, it lives; and what lives must grow. It is the law of nature. Turn me over, you stupid clod! Shake the net, or pull it up and turn me."

Well, the manners of the thing were very bad; but it occurred to me that I should probably feel irritable if my head had been lopped off; so I shook the net until the head turned upon one side so that it might look out away from the belly of the malagor.

"What are you called?" it asked.

"Vor Daj."

"I shall remember. In Morbus you may need a friend. I shall remember you."

"Thanks," I said. I wondered what good a friend without a body could do me. I also wondered if shaking the net for the thing would outweigh the fact that I had lopped its head off. Just to be polite, I asked what its name might be.

"I am Tor-dur-bar," it replied. "I am Tor-dur-bar, himself. You are very fortunate to have me for a friend. I am really outstanding. You will appreciate this when you come to Morbus and learn to know many of us hormads."

Tor-dur-bar is four-million-eight in the language of you Earthmen. It seemed a peculiar name, but then everything about these hormads was peculiar. The hormad in front of me had evidently been listening to our conversation, for he half turned his head; and said, disparagingly, "Pay no attention to Tor-dur-bar. He is an upstart. It is I who am remarkable. If you wish a powerful friend—well, you need look no farther. I cannot say more; I'm too modest. But if at any time you need a real friend, just come to Teeaytan-ov." (That is eleven-hundred-seven in your language.)

Tor-dur-bar scoffed disgustedly. " 'Upstart' indeed! I am the finished product of a million cultures, or more than four million cultures, to be exact. Teeaytan-ov is scarcely more than an experiment."

"If I should loosen my net, you would be a finished product," threatened Teeaytan-ov.

Tor-dur-bar commenced to scream, "Sytor! Sytor! Murder!"

The dwar, who had been flying at the head of his strange detachment, wheeled his malagor and flew back alongside us. "What's wrong here?" he demanded.

"Teeaytan-ov threatens to dump me into the Toonolian

Marshes," cried Tor-dur-bar. "Take me away from him, Sytor."

"Quarreling again, eh?" demanded Sytor. "If I hear any more out of either of you, you both go to the incinerator when we get back to Morbus; and, Teeaytan-ov, see that nothing happens to Tor-dur-bar. You understand?"

Teeaytan-ov grunted, and Sytor returned to his post. We rode on in silence after this, and I was left to speculate upon the origin of these strange creatures into whose hands I had fallen. The Warlord rode ahead of me and the girl a little to my left. My eyes wandered often in her direction; and my sympathy went out to her, for I was sure she, too, was a prisoner. To what terrible fate was she being borne? Our situation was quite bad enough for a man; I could only guess how much worse it might be for a woman.

The malagors flew swiftly and smoothly. My guess would be that they flew at a speed of more than four hundred haads a zode (about sixty miles an hour). They appeared tireless; and flew on, hour after hour, without rest. After circling Phundahl, we had flown due east; and late in the afternoon approached a large island rising from the surrounding morass. One of the innumerable winding waterways skirted its northern boundary, widening here to form a small lake on the shore of which lay a small walled city which we circled once before descending to a landing before its main gate, which faced the lake. During our descent, I had noticed clusters of small huts scattered about the island outside the walls of the city wherever I could see, suggesting a considerable population; and as I could see only a small portion of the island, which was of considerable extent, I received the impression that it was inhabited by an enormous number of people. I was later to learn that even my wildest guess could not have equalled the truth.

After we had dismounted, we three prisoners were herded together; the arms, legs, heads, and bodies which had been salvaged from our battle earlier in the day were slung in nets so that they could be easily carried; the gates swung open, and we entered into the city of Morbus.

The officer in charge of the gate was a quite normal appearing human being, but his warriors were grotesque, ill-favored hormads. The former exchanged greetings with Sytor, asked him a few questions about us, and then directed the bearers to take their gruesome burdens to "Reclamation Laboratory No. 3," after which Sytor led us away up the avenue that ran south from the gate. At the first intersection, the bearers turned off to the left with the mutilated bodies; and as they were leaving us a voice called out, "Do not forget, Vor Daj, that Tor-dur-bar is your friend and that Teeaytan-ov is little better than an experiment."

I glanced around to see the grisly head of Four-million-eight leering at me from the bottom of a net. "I shall not forget," I said; and I knew that I never should forget the horror of it even though I might wonder in what way a bodiless head might be of service, however friendly its intentions.

Morbus differed from any Martian city I had ever visited. The buildings were substantial and without ornamentation, but there was a certain dignity in the simplicity of their lines that lent them a beauty all their own. It gave the impression of being a new city laid out in accordance with some well conceived plan, every line of which spelled efficiency. I could not but wonder what purpose such a city could serve here in the depths of the Great Toonolian Marshes. Who would, by choice, live in such a remote and depressing environment? How could such a city exist without markets or commerce?

My speculations were interrupted by our arrival before a small doorway in a blank wall. Sytor pounded on the door with the hilt of his sword, whereupon a small panel was opened and a face appeared.

"I am Sytor, Dwar of the 10th Utan, 1st Dar of the 3rd Jed's Guard. I bring prisoners to await the pleasure of The Council of the Seven Jeds."

"How many?" asked the man at the wicket.

"Three—two men and a woman."

The door swung open, and Sytor motioned us to enter. He did not accompany us. We found ourselves in what was evidently a guardroom, as there were about twenty hormad warriors there in addition to the officer who had admitted us, who, like the other officers we had seen, was a normal red man like ourselves. He asked us our names, which he entered in a book with other information such as our vocations and the cities from which we came; and it was during this questioning that I learned the name of the girl. She was Janai; and she said that she came from Amhor, a city about seven hundred miles north of Morbus. It is a small city ruled by a prince named Jal Had who has such a bad reputation that it has reached to far away Helium. That was about all that I knew about Amhor.

After he had finished questioning us, the officer directed one of the hormads to take us away; and we were led down a corridor to a large patio in which there were a number of

20

red Martians. "You will stay here until you are sent for," said the hormad. "Do not try to escape." Then he left us.

"Escape!" said John Carter with a wry smile. "I have escaped from many places; and I can probably escape from this city, but escaping from the Toonolian Marshes is another matter. However, we shall see."

The other prisoners, for such they proved to be, approached us. There were five of them. "Kaor!" they greeted us. We exchanged names; and they asked us many questions about the outside world, as though they had been prisoners for years. But they had not. The fact that Morbus was so isolated seemed to impart to them the feeling that they had been out of the world for a long time. Two of them were Phundahlians, one was from Toonol, one from Ptarth, and one from Duhor.

"For what purpose do they keep prisoners?" asked John Carter.

"They use some as officers to train and command their warriors," explained Pandar, one of the Phundahlians. "The bodies of others are used to house the brains of those of the hormads intelligent enough to serve in high places. The bodies of others go to the culture laboratories, where their tissue is used in the damnable work of Ras Thavas."

"Ras Thavas!" exclaimed The Warlord. "He is here in Morbus?"

"He is that—a prisoner in his own city, the servant of the hideous creatures he has created," replied Gan Had of Toonol.

"I don't follow you," said John Carter.

"After Ras Thavas was driven from his great laboratories by Vobis Kan, Jeddak of Toonol," explained Gan Had, "he came to this island to perfect a discovery he had been working on for years. It was the creation of human beings from human tissue. He had perfected a culture in which tissue grew continuously. The growth from a tiny particle of living tissue filled an entire room in his laboratory, but it was formless. His problem was to direct this growth. He experimented with various reptiles which reproduce certain parts of their bodies, such as toes, tails, and limbs, when they are cut off; and eventually he discovered the principle. This he has applied to the control of the growth of human tissue in a highly specialized culture. The result of these discoveries and experiments are the hormads. Seventy-five per cent of the buildings in Morbus are devoted to the culture and

21

growth of these horrid creatures which Ras Thavas turns out in enormous numbers.

"Practically all of them are extremely low in intelligence; but a few developed normal brains, and some of these banded together to take over the island and establish a kingdom of their own. On threat of death, they have compelled Ras Thavas to continue to produce these creatures in great numbers; for they have conceived a stupendous plan which is nothing less than to build up an army of millions of hormads and with them conquer the world. They will take Phundahl and Toonol first, and then gradually spread out over the entire surface of the globe."

"Amazing," said John Carter, "but I think they have reckoned without a full understanding of all the problems such an undertaking will involve. It is inconceivable, for instance, that Barsoom could feed such an army in the field; and this little island certainly could not feed the nucleus of such an army."

"There you are mistaken," replied Gan Had. "The food for the hormads is produced by means almost identical with those which produce them—a slightly different culture; that is all. Animal tissue grows with great rapidity in this culture, which can be carried along with an army in tanks, constantly providing sufficient food; and, because of its considerable water content, sufficient water."

"But can these half-humans hope to be victorious over well trained, intelligent troops fitted for modern warfare?" I asked.

"I think so," said Pandar. "They will do it by their overwhelming numbers, their utter fearlessness, and the fact that it is necessary to decapitate them before they can be rendered *hors de combat*."

"How large an army have they?" inquired John Carter.

"There are several million hormads on the island. Their huts are scattered over the entire area of Morbus. It is estimated that the island can accommodate a hundred million of them; and Ras Thavas claims that he can march them into battle at the rate of two million a year, lose every one of them, and still have his original strength undepleted by as much as a single man. This plant turns them out in enormous quantities. A certain percentage are so grossly malformed as to be utterly useless. These are sliced into hundreds of thousands of tiny pieces that are dumped back into the culture vats, where they grow with such unbelievable rapidity that within nine days each has developed into a full-sized hormad, an amazing number of which have developed into something that can march and wield a weapon."

"The situation would appear serious but for one thing," said John Carter.

"And what is that?" asked Gan Had.

"Transportation. How are they going to transport such an enormous army?"

"That has been their problem, but they believe that Ras Thavas has now solved it. He has been experimenting for a long time with malagor tissue and a special culture medium. If he can produce these birds in sufficient quantities, the problem of transport will have been solved. For the fighting ships which they will need, they are relying on those they expect to capture when they take Phundahl and Toonol as the nucleus of a great fleet which will grow as their conquests take in more and larger cities."

The conversation was interrupted by the arrival of a couple of hormads carrying a vessel which contained animal tissue for our evening meal—a most unappetizing looking mess.

The prisoner from Duhor, who, it seemed, had volunteered to act as cook, built a fire in the oven that formed a part of the twenty foot wall that closed the only side of the patio that was not surrounded by portions of the building; and presently our dinner was grilling over a hot fire.

I could not contemplate the substance of our meal without a feeling of revulsion, notwithstanding the fact that I was ravenously hungry; and my mind was alive with doubts engendered by all that I had been listening to since entering the compound; so that I turned to Gan Had with a question. "Is this, by any chance, human tissue?" I asked.

He shrugged. "It is not supposed to be; but that is a question we do not even ask ourselves, for we must eat to live; and this is all that they bring us."

CHAPTER V

THE JUDGMENT OF THE JEDS

JANAI, THE GIRL from Amhor, sat apart. Her situation seemed to me pathetic in the extreme—a lone woman incarcerated with seven strange men in a city of hideous enemies. We red men of Barsoom are naturally a chivalrous race; but men are men, and I knew nothing of the five whom we had

23

found here. As long as John Carter and I remained her fellow prisoners she would be safe; that I knew, and I thought that if she knew it, any burden of apprehension she might be carrying would be lightened.

As I approached her, with the intention of entering into conversation with her, the officer who had questioned us in the guardroom entered the compound with two other officers and several hormads. They gathered us together, and the two officers accompanying the officer of the guard looked us over. "Not a bad lot," said one.

The other shrugged. "The jeds will take the best of them, and Ras Thavas will grumble about the material he is getting. He always does."

"They don't want the girl, do they?" asked the officer of the guard.

"Our orders were to bring the prisoners," replied one of the others.

"I should like to keep the girl," said the officer of the guard.

"Who wouldn't?" demanded the other with a laugh. "If she had the face of an ulsio you might get her; but the good looking ones go to the jeds, and she is more than good looking."

Janai was standing next to me, and I could almost feel her shudder. Moved by a sudden impulse, I pressed her hand; and for an instant she clung to mine, instinctively groping for protection; then she dropped it and flushed.

"I wish I might help you," I said.

"You are kind. I understand, but no one can help. You are only better off in that you are a man. The worst they will do to you is kill you."

The hideous hormads surrounded us, and we were marched back through the guardroom and out into the avenue. John Carter asked an officer where we were being taken.

"To the Council of the Seven Jeds," he said. "There it will be determined what disposition is to be made of you. Some of you will go into the culture vats. Those of you who are fortunate will be retained to train and officer troops as I was. It's not much to look forward to, but it's better than death."

"What is the Council of the Seven Jeds?" asked The Warlord.

"They are the rulers of Morbus. They are the seven hormads whose brains developed normally and who wrested control from Ras Thavas. Each one aspired to rule; and as

24

none would give up what he considered his rights, they proclaimed themselves all jeds, and rule conjointly."

At a little distance from our prison we came to a large building before the entrance to which was a guard of hormad warriors commanded by a couple of officers. There was a brief parley here, and then we were taken into the building and along a long corridor to a large chamber before the doorway to which we were detained for a few minutes by another detail of guardsmen. When the door was opened we saw a number of hormads and officers standing about and at the far end of the room a raised dais on which seven red men were seated on carved chairs. These were evidently the seven jeds, but they did not look like the hormads we had previously seen. On the contrary they were quite normal and most of them fine looking men.

We were taken to the foot of the dais; and here they looked us over, asking about the same questions that the officer of the guard had asked us when we were admitted to the prison. They discussed us at some length, as men might discuss a number of thoats or calots they were considering purchasing. Several of them seemed much interested in Janai, and finally three of them laid claim to her. This started an altercation which ended in a vote being taken as to which of them would get her, but as there was never a majority in favor of any one man, it was decided to hold her for a few days and then turn her over to Ras Thavas if the claimants could not come to some agreement among themselves. This decided, one of the jeds addressed us men prisoners.

"How many of you will serve us as officers of our troops if you are permitted to live?" he asked.

The only alternative being death, we all proclaimed our willingness to serve as officers. The jeds nodded. "We shall now determine which of you are best fitted to serve as officers of our fighting men," said one; and, speaking to an officer standing near us: "Fetch seven of our best warriors."

We were then led to one side of the room, where we waited. "It looks like fighting," said John Carter with a smile.

"I am sure that nothing would suit you better," I replied.

"Nor you," he said; then he turned to the officer with whom he had talked on the way from the prison. "I thought you said the seven jeds were hormads," he said.

"They are."

"They don't look like any of the hormads I have seen."

"Ras Thavas fixed them up," said the officer. "Perhaps you

25

don't know that Ras Thavas is the greatest scientist and surgeon on Barsoom."

"I have heard as much."

"You have heard right. He can take your brain out and put it in the skull of another man. He has performed that operation hundreds of times. When the seven jeds heard about it they selected seven of the best looking officers and compelled Ras Thavas to transfer their brains into the skulls of these officers. You see they had been hideous creatures, and they wanted to be handsome."

"And the seven officers?" I asked.

"They went to the culture vats, or rather their brains did —the original bodies of the seven jeds went with them. Here come the seven fighting warriors. In a few minutes you will know which of you are going into the vats."

We were now taken to the center of the room and lined up facing seven huge hormads. These were the least malformed that we had so far seen, but they were still most repulsive looking creatures. We were furnished with swords, and an officer gave us our instructions. Each of us was to engage the hormad facing him, and those of us who survived without a serious wound would be permitted to live and serve as officers in the army of Morbus.

At a command from an officer, the two lines advanced; and in an instant the chamber rang with the clash of steel on steel. We men of Helium believe that we are the best swordsmen on Barsoom, and of us all, none is so great a swordsman as John Carter; so I had no apprehensions as to the outcome of the contest so far as he and I were concerned. The creature attacking me depended upon weight and brute strength to overcome me, which are the tactics most generally adopted by all of them, since they are not endowed with any great amount of intelligence. He evidently hoped to cut through my guard with a single terrific stroke of his heavy weapon, but of course I am too old a hand at fighting to fall victim to any such crude method of attack. As I parried his cut and stepped aside, he rushed past me awkwardly; and I could have run him through easily, but I had learned in my first encounter with these monsters that what would constitute a lethal wound to a mortal man would cause a hormad no inconvenience whatsoever. I should have to sever one of his legs or both his arms or decapitate him to put him out of the fighting. That, of course, gave him a tremendous advantage over me; but it was not insuperable. Or at least that was what I thought at the beginning of our

26

engagement, but I soon commenced to have a suggestion of a doubt. The fellow was a far better swordsman than any of those we had encountered at the time of our capture. As I learned later, these creatures against whom we were pitted were selected for their superior intelligence, which was slightly above the average of their kind, and specially schooled in swordsmanship by red Martian officers.

Of course, had he been a normal man I could have easily dispatched him; but to avoid his mad rushes and his blade and decapitate him presently appeared a much larger job than I had anticipated. Aside from all else, he was a most unpleasant antagonist, for his face was absolutely hideous. One eye was far up at the corner of his forehead and twice as large as its mate. His nose had grown where one of his ears should have been, while his ear occupied the normal position of his nose. His mouth was a large and crooked rent filled with great fangs. His countenance alone might have been quite enough to have unmanned an antagonist.

Occasionally I caught a glimpse of the other duels progressing around me. I saw one of the Phundahlians fall, and almost simultaneously the head of John Carter's antagonist rolled upon the floor where it lay cursing and screaming while its body lunged madly about endangering everyone in the chamber. A number of other hormads and officers pursued it with nooses and nets in an effort to catch and bind it, and while they were thus occupied the thing bumped into my antagonist throwing it off balance and giving me the opening for which I had been waiting. I swung a terrific blow then and caught the fellow square across the neck, sending his head rolling upon the floor. Then there were two headless bodies dashing about hacking right and left with their heavy swords. I tell you, the other hormads and the officers had a busy few minutes before they finally captured and subdued the horrible things; and by the time they had the fighting was over, but there were two more hormads flopping about the floor, each with a leg gone. These had been overcome by Pandar and Gan Had. The man from Ptarth and the man from Duhor had been killed. Only four of us seven were left. The two heads upon the floor reviled us while other hormads gathered up the debris of battle and carried it away in nets.

Now we were taken again before the dais of the Council of the Seven Jeds; and once more they questioned us, but this time more carefully. When they had done with the questioning they whispered among themselves for a while; then one of them addressed us.

"You will serve as officers, obeying your superiors and all orders you may receive from the Council of the Seven Jeds," he said. "You cannot escape from Morbus. If you serve faithfully you will be permitted to live. If you are guilty of disobedience or treason you will be sent to the vats. That will be the end of you." He turned to John Carter and me. "You men from Helium will serve for the present with the laboratory guard. It is the duty of the laboratory guard to see that Ras Thavas does not escape and that no harm befalls him. We have chosen you for this duty for two reasons: you are both extraordinary swordsmen and, being from distant Helium, cannot feel any partiality either for him or for Toonol or for Phundahl. You can therefore act wholly in our interests as against those of these enemies. Ras Thavas would like to escape or regain control of Morbus. Phundahl would like to rescue him. Toonol would like to destroy him. Either one of them would be glad to get him away from us so that he could produce no more hormads. The man from Phundahl and the man from Toonol will be used to train our warriors as they emerge from the vats. The Council of the Seven Jeds has spoken; it is for you to obey." He nodded toward the officer who had brought us in. "Take them away."

I looked toward Janai. She caught my eye and smiled at me. It was a very brave little smile. A pathetic little smile out of a hopeless heart. Then they led us away.

CHAPTER VI

RAS THAVAS, MASTER MIND OF MARS

As THEY CONDUCTED us down the corridor toward the main entrance to the building my mind was occupied in reviewing the incredible occurrences of the day. These few hours had encompassed a lifetime. I had passed through such adventures as in my wildest dreams I could not have imagined. I had become an officer in the hideous army of a city the very existence of which I had not dreamed of a few hours ago. I had met a strange girl from far Amhor; and, for the first time in my life, I had fallen in love; and almost within the hour I had lost her. Love is a strange thing. Why it had come to me as it had, how it had come, were quite beyond me to explain. I only knew that I loved Janai, that I should always love her. I should never see her again. I should never know if I might have won her love in return. I should never be able to tell her that I loved her. My whole life hereafter would be colored and saddened by the thought of my love, by my remembrance of her; yet I would not have relinquished my love for her could I have done so. Yes, love is a strange thing.

At the intersection of the main corridor with another, John Carter and I were led to the right. Pandar and Gan Had continued on toward the main entrance. We called goodbye to one another and were gone. It is remarkable how quickly friendships are formed in the midst of a common jeopardy. These men were from strange cities commonly enemies of Helium, yet because we had endured danger together I felt a definite friendly attachment toward them; and I did not doubt but that they were inclined similarly toward John Carter and me. I wondered if we should ever meet again.

They led us down this new corridor and across a great courtyard into another building, above the entrance to which were hieroglyphics strange to me. No two nations of Barsoom have the same written language, although there is a common scientific language understood by the savants of all nations; yet there is but one spoken language upon Barsoom, which all peoples use and understand, even the savage green men of the dead sea bottom. But John Carter is very learned and reads many languages. He told me that the hieroglyphics read Laboratory Building.

We were taken into a medium size audience chamber where an officer told us to wait and that he would fetch Ras Thavas, that we might meet the man we were to help guard and watch. He also told us that Ras Thavas was to be treated with respect and consideration as long as he made no effort to escape. He had the freedom of the laboratory and was, in a sense, all powerful there. If he called on us to help him in his work, we were to do so. It was evident that the Council of the Seven Jeds looked with awe upon him although he was their prisoner, and that they had sense enough to make life as easy for him as possible. I was very anxious to see Ras Thavas, of whom I had heard. He was called The Master Mind of Mars, and although he had often turned his remarkable talents to nefarious schemes, he was nevertheless admired because of his great learning and skill. He was known to be over a thousand years old; and because of this fact alone I would have been curious to see him, as the span of life upon Barsoom is seldom so great. A thousand years is supposed to be the limit, but because of our warlike natures and the prevalency of assassination few attain it. He must, indeed, have been a withered little mummy of a man, I thought; and I wondered that he had the strength to carry on the enormous work in which he was engaged.

We had waited but a short time when the officer returned accompanied by an extremely handsome young man who looked at us with a haughty and supercilious air, as though we had been the dregs of humanity and he a god.

"Two more spies to watch me," he sneered.

"Two more fighting men to protect you, Ras Thavas," corrected the officer who had brought us here from the other building.

So this was Ras Thavas! I could not believe my eyes. This was a young man, unquestionably; for while it is true that we Martians show few traces of advancing years until almost the end of our allotted span, at which time decay is rapid, yet there are certain indications of youth that are obvious.

Ras Thavas continued to scrutinize us. I saw his brows contract in thought as his eyes held steadily on John Carter as though he were trying to recall a half remembered face. Yet I knew that these two men had never met. What was in the mind of Ras Thavas?

"How do I know," he suddenly snapped, "that they have not wormed their way into Morbus to assassinate me? How do I know that they are not from Toonol or Phundahl?"

"They are from Helium," replied the officer. I saw Ras Thavas's brow clear as though he had suddenly arrived at the solution of a problem. "They are two panthans whom we found on their way to Phundahl seeking service," concluded the officer.

Ras Thavas nodded. "I shall use them to assist me in the laboratory," he said.

The officer looked surprised. "Had they not better serve in the guard for a while?" he suggested, "That will give you time to have them watched and to determine if it would be safe to have them possibly alone with you in the laboratory."

"I know what I am doing," snapped Ras Thavas. "I don't

need the assistance of any fifth-rate brain to decide what is best for me. But perhaps I honor you."

The officer flushed. "My orders were simply to turn these men over to you. How you use them is none of my concern. I merely wished to safeguard you."

"Then carry out your orders and mind your own business. I can take care of myself." His tone was as disagreeable as his words. I had a premonition that he was not going to be a very pleasant person with whom to work.

The officer shrugged, gave a command to the hormad warriors that had accompanied us, and marched them from the audience chamber. Ras Thavas nodded to us. "Come with me," he said. He led us to a small room, the walls of which were entirely lined with shelves packed with books and manuscripts. There was a desk littered with papers and books, at which he seated himself, at the same time motioning us to be seated at a bench nearby.

"By what names do you call yourselves?" he asked.

"I am Dotar Sojat," replied John Carter, "and this is Vor Daj."

"You know Vor Daj well and have implicit confidence in him?" demanded Ras Thavas. It seemed a strange question, since Ras Thavas knew neither of us.

"I have known Vor Daj for years," replied The Warlord. "I would trust to his loyalty and intelligence in any matter and to his skill and courage as a warrior."

"Very well," said Ras Thavas; "then I can trust you both."

"But how do you know you can trust me?" inquired John Carter quizzically.

Ras Thavas smiled. "The integrity of John Carter, Prince of Helium, Warlord of Barsoom, is a matter of worldwide knowledge," he said.

We looked at him in surprise. "What makes you think I am John Carter?" asked The Warlord. "You have never seen him."

"In the audience chamber I was struck by the fact that you did not appear truly a red Martian. I examined you more closely and discovered that the pigment with which you had stained your skin had worn thin in spots. There are but two inhabitants of Jasoom on Mars. One of them is Vad Varo, whose Earth name was Paxton. I know him well, as he served as my assistant in my laboratories in Toonol. In fact it was he whom I trained to such a degree of skill that he was able to transfer my old brain to this young body. So I knew that you were not Vad Varo. The

31

other Jasoomian being John Carter, the deduction was simple."

"Your suspicions were well founded and your reasoning faultless," said The Warlord. "I am John Carter. I should soon have told you so myself, for I was on my way to Phundahl in search of you when we were captured by the hormads."

"And for what reason did The Warlord of Barsoom search for Ras Thavas?" demanded the great surgeon.

"My princess, Dejah Thoris, was badly injured in a collision between two fliers. She has lain unconscious for many days The greatest surgeons of Helium are powerless to aid her. I sought Ras Thavas to implore his aid in restoring her to health."

"And now you find me a prisoner on a remote island in the Great Toonolian Marshes—a fellow prisoner with you."

"But I have found you."

"And what good will it do you or your princess?" demanded The Master Mind of Mars.

"You would come with me and help her if you could?" asked John Carter.

"Certainly. I promised Vad Varo and Dar Tarus, Jeddak of Phundahl, that I would dedicate my skill and knowledge to the amelioration of suffering and the betterment of mankind."

"Then we shall find a way," said John Carter.

Ras Thavas shook his head. "It is easy to say, but impossible to accomplish. There can be no escape from Morbus."

"Still we must find a way," replied The Warlord. "I foresee that the difficulties of escaping from the island may not be insuperable. It is travelling the Great Toonolian Marshes that gives me the greatest concern."

Ras Thavas shook his head. "We can never get off the island. It is too well patrolled, for one thing; and there are too many spies and informers. Many of the officers who appear to be red Martians are, in reality, hormads whose brains I have been forced to transfer to the bodies of normal men. Not even I know who these are, as the operations were performed only in the presence of the Council of the Seven Jeds; and the faces of the red men were kept masked. They have cunning minds, some of these seven jeds. They wanted those they could trust to spy upon me, and if I had seen the faces of the red Martians to whom I gave hormad brains their plan would have been ineffective. Now

I do not know which of the officers surrounding me are hormads and which are normal men—except two. I am sure of John Carter because I would have known had I performed a brain transfer on a man with the white skin of a Jasoomian; and I have John Carter's word as to you, Vor Daj. Beyond us three there is none we may trust; so be careful with whom you become friendly and what you say in the hearing of others. You will——"

Here he was interrupted by a veritable pandemonium that suddenly broke out in another part of the building. It seemed a horrific medley of screams and bellowings and groans and grunts, as though a horde of wild beasts had suddenly gone berserk.

"Come," said Ras Thavas, "to the spawning of the monsters. We may be needed."

CHAPTER VII

THE VATS OF LIFE

RAS THAVAS LED us to an enormous room where we beheld such a spectacle as probably never had been enacted elsewhere in the entire universe. In the center of the room was a huge tank about four feet high from which were emerging hideous monstrosities almost beyond the powers of human imagination to conceive; and surrounding the tank were a great number of hormad warriors with their officers, rushing upon the terrible creatures, overpowering and binding them, or destroying them if they were too malformed to function successfully as fighting men. At least fifty per centum of them had to be thus destroyed—fearful caricatures of life that were neither beast nor man. One was only a great mass of living flesh with an eye somewhere and a single hand. Another had developed with its arms and legs transposed, so that when it walked it was upside down with its head between its legs. The features of many were grotesquely misplaced. Noses, ears, eyes, mouths might be scattered indiscriminately anywhere over the surfaces of torso or limbs. These were all destroyed; only those were preserved which had two arms and legs and the facial features of which were somewhere upon the head. The nose might be under an ear and the mouth above the eyes, but if they could function appearance was of no importance.

Ras Thavas viewed them with evident pride. "What do you think of them?" he asked The Warlord.

"Quite horrible," replied John Carter.

Ras Thavas appeared hurt. "I have made no attempt as yet to attain beauty," he said; "and I shall have to admit that so far even symmetry has eluded me, but both will come. I have created human beings. Some day I shall create the perfect man, and a new race of supermen will inhabit Barsoom—beautiful, intelligent, deathless."

"And in the meantime these creatures will have spread all over the world and conquered it. They will destroy your supermen. You have created a Frankensteinian host that will not only destroy you but the civilization of a world. Hasn't that possibility ever occurred to you?"

"Yes, it has; but I never intended to create these creatures in any such numbers. That is the idea of the seven jeds. I purposed developing only enough to form a small army with which to conquer Toonol, that I might regain my island and my old laboratory."

The din in the room had now risen to such proportions that further conversation was impossible. Screaming heads rolled upon the floor. Hormad warriors dragged away the newly created creatures that were considered fit to live, and fresh warriors swarmed into the chamber to replace them. New hormads emerged constantly from the culture tank which swarmed with writhing life like an enormous witch's pot. And this same scene was being duplicated in forty similar rooms throughout the city of Morbus, while a stream of new hormads was pouring out of the city to be tamed and trained by officers and the more intelligent hormads.

I was delighted and relieved when Ras Thavas suggested that we inspect another phase of his work and we were permitted to leave that veritable chamber of horrors. He took us to another room where reconstruction work was carried on. Here heads were growing new bodies and headless bodies new heads. Hormads which had lost arms or legs were growing new ones. Sometimes these activities went amiss, when nothing but a single leg sprouted from the neck of a severed head. An identical case was among those that we saw in this room. The head was very angry about it, and became quite abusive, reviling Ras Thavas.

"What good shall I be," he demanded, "with only a head and one leg? They call you The Master Mind of Mars! Phooey! You haven't the brains of a sorak. When they produce their kind they give them a body and six legs, to

34

say nothing of a head. Now what are you going to do about it? That's what I want to know."

"Well," said Ras Thavas, thoughtfully, "I can always re-disect you and return the pieces to the culture vat."

"No! No!" screamed the head. "Let me live, but cut off this leg and let me try to grow a body."

"Very well," said Ras Thavas; "tomorrow."

"Why should a thing like that wish to live," I asked, after we had passed along.

"It is a characteristic of life, however low its form," replied Ras Thavas. "Even these poor sexless monstrosities, whose only pleasure in life is eating raw animal tissue, wish to live. They do not even dream of the existence of love or friendship, they have no spiritual or mental resources upon which to draw for satisfaction or enjoyment; yet they wish to live."

"They speak of friendship," I said. "Tor-dur-bar's head told me not to forget that it was my friend."

"They know the word," replied Ras Thavas, "but I am sure they cannot sense its finer connotations. One of the first things they are taught is to obey. Perhaps he meant that he would obey you, serve you. He may not even remember you now. Some of them have practically no memories. All their reactions are purely mechanical. They respond to oft repeated stimuli—the commands to march, to fight, to come, to go, to halt. They also do what they see the majority of their fellows doing. Come! We shall find Tor-dur-bar's head and see if it recalls you. It will be an interesting experiment."

We passed into another chamber where reconstruction work was in progress, and Ras Thavas spoke to an officer in charge there. The man led us to the far end of the room where there was a large vat in which torsos were growing new arms or legs or heads, and several heads growing new bodies.

We had no more than reached the tank when a head cried out, "Kaor, Vor Daj!" It was Four-Million-Eight himself.

"Kaor, Tor-dur-bar!" I replied. "I am glad to see you again."

"Don't forget that you have one friend in Morbus," he said. "Soon I shall have a new body, and then if you need me I shall be ready."

"There is a hormad of unusual intelligence," said Ras Thavas. "I shall have to keep an eye on him."

"You should give such a brain as mine a fine looking body," said Tor-dur-bar. "I should like to be as handsome as Vor Daj or his friend."

"We shall see," said Ras Thavas, and then he leaned close and whispered to the head, "Say no more about it now. Just trust me."

"How long will it take to grow a new body for Tor-dur-bar?" John Carter asked.

"Nine days; but it may be a body he can't use, and then it will have to be done over again. I have accomplished much, but I still cannot control the development of these bodies or any part of them. Ordinarily his head will grow a body. It might be a body so malformed as to be useless, or it might be just a part of a body or even another head. Some day I shall be able to control this. Some day I shall be able to create perfect humans."

"If there is an Almighty God he may resent this usurpation of his prerogatives," remarked The Warlord with a smile.

"The origin of life is an obscure mystery," said Ras Thavas, "and there is quite as much evidence to indicate that it was the result of accident as there is to suggest that it was planned by a supreme being. I understand that the scientists of your Earth believe that all life on that planet was evolved from a very low form of animal life called amoeba, a microscopic nucleated mass of protoplasm without even a rudimentary form of consciousness or mental life. An omnipotent creator could just as well have produced the highest conceivable form of life in the first place —a perfect creature—whereas no existing life on either planet is perfect or even approximates perfection.

"Now, on Mars, we hold to a very different theory of creation and evolution. We believe that as the planet cooled chemicals combined to form a spore which was the basis of vegetable life from which, after countless ages, the Tree of Life grew and flourished, perhaps in the center of the Valley Dor twenty-three million years ago, as some believe, perhaps elsewhere. For countless ages the fruit of this tree underwent the gradual changes of evolution, passing by degrees from true plant life to a combination of plant and animal. In the first stages, the fruit of the tree possessed only the power of independent muscular action, while the stem remained attached to the parent plant; later, a brain developed in the fruit, so that hanging there by their long stems they thought and moved as individuals. Then, with the development of perception came a comparison of them; judgments were reached and compared, and thus reason and the power to reason were born upon Barsoom.

"Ages passed. Many forms of life came and went upon the Tree of Life, but still all were attached to the parent plant by stems of varying lengths. At length, the fruit upon the tree consisted of tiny plant men, such as may now be found reproduced in huge size in the Valley Dor, but still hanging to the limbs and branches of The Tree by the stems which grew from the tops of their heads.

"The buds from which the plant men blossomed resembled large nuts about a foot in diameter, divided by double partition walls into four sections. In one section grew the plant man, in another a six legged worm, in the third the progenitor of the white ape, and in the fourth the primeval human of Barsoom. When the bud burst, the plant man remained dangling at the end of his stem; but the three other sections fell to the ground, where the efforts of their imprisoned occupants to escape sent them hopping about in all directions.

"Thus, as time went on, these imprisoned creatures were scattered far and wide over the surface of the planet. For ages they lived their long lives within their hard shells, hopping and skipping hither and thither, falling into the rivers, lakes, and seas which then existed upon the surface of Barsoom, to be still further spread across the face of the new world. Countless billions died before the first human broke through his prison walls into the light of day. Prompted by curiosity, he broke open other shells; and the peopling of Barsoom commenced. The Tree of Life is dead, but before it died the plant men learned to detach themselves from it, their bisexuality permitting them to reproduce themselves after the manner of true plants."

"I have seen them in the Valley Dor," said John Carter, "with a tiny plant man growing beneath each arm, dangling like fruit from the stems attached to the tops of their heads."

"Thus, casually, the present forms of life evolved," continued Ras Thavas, "and by studying them all from the lowest forms upward I have learned how to reproduce life."

"Perhaps to your sorrow," I suggested.

"Perhaps," he agreed.

CHAPTER VIII

THE RED ASSASSIN

DAYS PASSED DURING which Ras Thavas kept us almost constantly with him; but almost invariably there were others around, so that we had few opportunities to plan, as we never knew the friend from the spy. Thoughts of Janai filled me with sorrow, and I was ever watchful for some means whereby I might learn her fate. Ras Thavas warned me not to show too much interest in the girl, as it might result in arousing suspicions that would lead to my destruction; but he assured me that he would aid me in any way that he could that would not lay me open to suspicion, and one day he found the means.

A number of unusually intelligent hormads were to be sent before the Council of the Seven Jeds to be examined as to their fitness to serve in the personal body guards which each jed maintained, and Ras Thavas detailed me with other officers to accompany them. It was the first time I had been outside the laboratory building, as none of us was permitted to leave it other than on some official business such as this.

As I entered the great building, which was in effect the palace of the Seven Jeds, my whole mind was occupied with thoughts of Janai and the hope that I might catch a glimpse of her. I looked down corridors, I peered through open doorways, I even considered leaving the party and concealing myself in one of the rooms we passed and then attempting a search of the palace; but my better judgment came to my rescue, and I continued on with the others to the great chamber where the Council of the Seven Jeds sat.

The examination of the hormads was very thorough, and while listening to it carefully and noting every question and answer and the effect of the answers upon the jeds, the seeds of a plan were planted in my mind. If I could get Tor-dur-bar assigned to the body guard of a jed I might thus learn the fate of Janai. How differently it worked out and what a bizarre plan finally developed, you shall learn in time.

While we were still in the council chamber a number of warriors entered with a prisoner, a swaggering red man, a scarred, hard bitten warrior, whose sneering face and haughty, arrogant manner seemed a deliberate, studied affront to his captors and the seven jeds. He was a powerful man, and despite the efforts of the warriors with him he forced his way almost to the foot of the dais before they could restrain him.

"Who is this man?" demanded one of the jeds.

"I am Gantun Gur, the assassin of Amhor," bellowed the captive in a great voice. "Give me back my sword, you stinking ulsios, and let me show you what a real fighting man can do to these deformed monstrosities of yours and to you, too. They caught me in nets, which is no way for decent men to take a warrior."

"Silence!" commanded a jed, pale with anger, and smarting under the insult of being called an ill smelling rat.

"Silence?" screamed Gantun Gur. "By my first ancestor! There lives no man can make Gantun Gur keep silent. Come down here and try it, man to man, you snivelling worm."

"Off with him!" cried the jed. "Take him to Ras Thavas, and tell Ras Thavas to take out his brain and burn it. He can do what he pleases with the body."

Gantun Gur fought like a demon, knocking hormads to right and left; and they only subdued him at last by entangling him in their nets. Then, bellowing curses and insults, he was dragged away toward the laboratory.

Shortly thereafter the jeds selected the hormads they chose to retain, and we conducted the others out of the chamber, where they were turned over to officers to be assigned to such duties as they were considered equal to. Then I returned to the laboratory building without having had a glimpse of Janai or learning anything concerning her. I was terribly disappointed and despondent.

I found Ras Thavas in his small private study. John Carter and a fairly well formed hormad were with him. The latter was standing with his back toward me as I entered the room. When he heard my voice he turned and greeted me by name. It was Tor-dur-bar with his newly grown body. One arm was a little longer than the other, his torso was out of proportion to his short legs, and he had six toes on one foot and an extra thumb on his left hand; but, altogether, he was a pretty good specimen for a hormad.

"Well, here I am as good as new," he exclaimed, a broad grin splitting his horrid countenance. "What do you think of me?"

"I'm glad to have you as a friend," I said. "I think that new body of yours is very powerful. It's splendidly muscled." And indeed it was.

"I should, however, like a body and face like yours," said Tor-dur-bar. "I was just talking to Ras Thavas about it, and he has promised to get me one, if he can."

Instantly I recalled Gantun Gur, the assassin of Amhor, and the doom that had been pronounced upon him by the jed. "I think a good body is waiting for you in the laboratory," I said; then I told them the story of Gantun Gur. "Now it is up to Ras Thavas. The jed said he could do what he pleased with the body."

"We'll have a look at the man," said The Master Mind of Mars, and led the way out toward the reception room where new victims were held pending his orders.

We found Gantun Gur securely trussed up and heavily guarded. At sight of us he commenced to bellow and rail, insulting all three of us indiscriminately. He appeared to have a most evil disposition. Ras Thavas regarded him for a moment in silence; then he dismissed the warriors and officers who had brought him.

"We will take care of him," he said. "Report to the Council of the Seven Jeds that his brain will be burned and his body put to some good use."

At that, Gantun Gur broke into such a tirade that I thought he had gone mad, and perhaps he had. He gnashed his teeth and foamed at the mouth and called Ras Thavas everything he could lay his tongue to.

Ras Thavas turned to Tor-dur-bar. "Can you carry him?" he asked.

For answer, the hormad picked up the red man as easily as though he had no weight and flung him across one broad shoulder. Tor-dur-bar's new body was indeed a mountain of strength.

Ras Thavas led the way back to his private study and through a small doorway into a chamber that I had not seen before. Here were two tables standing about twenty inches apart, the top of each a beautifully polished slab of solid ersite. At one end of the tables was a shelf on which were two empty glass vessels and two similar vessels filled with a clear, colorless liquid resembling water. Beneath each table was a small motor. There were numerous surgical instruments neatly arranged, various vessels containing colored liquids, and paraphernalia such as one might find in a laboratory or hospital concerning the uses of which I knew nothing, for I am, first and last, a fighting man and nothing else.

Ras Thavas directed Tor-dur-bar to lay Gantun Gur on

40

one of the tables. "Now get on the other one yourself," he said.

"You are really going to do it?" exclaimed Tor-dur-bar. "You are going to give me a beautiful new body and face?"

"I wouldn't call it particularly beautiful," said Ras Thavas, with a slight smile.

"Oh, it is lovely," cried Tor-dur-bar. "I shall be your slave forever if you do this for me."

Although Gantun Gur was securely bound, it took both John Carter and myself to hold him still while Ras Thavas made two incisions in his body, one in a large vein and one in an artery. To these incisions he attached the ends of two tubes, one of which was connected with an empty glass receptacle and the other to the similar receptacle containing the colorless liquid. The connections made, he pressed a button controlling the small motor beneath the table, and Gantun Gur's blood was pumped into the empty jar while the contents of the other jar were forced into the emptying veins and arteries. Of course Gantun Gur lost consciousness almost immediately after the motor was started, and I breathed a sigh of relief when I had heard the last of him. When all the blood had been replaced by the colorless liquid, Ras Thavas removed the tubes and closed the openings in the body with bits of adhesive material; then he turned to Tor-dur-bar.

"You're quite sure you want to be a red man?" he asked.

"I can't wait," replied the hormad.

Ras Thavas repeated the operation he had just performed on Gantun Gur; then he sprayed both bodies with what he told us was a strong antiseptic solution and then himself, scrubbing his hands thoroughly. He now selected a sharp knife from among the instruments and removed the scalps from both bodies, following the hair line entirely around each head. This done, he sawed through the skull of each with a tiny circular saw attached to the end of a flexible, revolving shaft, following the line he had exposed by the removal of the scalps.

It was a long and marvelously skillful operation that followed, and at the end of four hours he had transferred the brain of Tor-dur-bar to the brain pan of him who had been Gantun Gur, deftly connected the severed nerves and ganglia, replaced the skull and scalp and bound the head securely with adhesive material, which was not only antiseptic and healing but locally anaesthetic as well.

He now reheated the blood he had drawn from Gantun Gur's body, adding a few drops of some clear chemical solution, and as he withdrew the liquid from the veins and arteries he pumped the blood back to replace it. Immediately following this he administered a hypodermic injection.

"In an hour," he said, "Tor-dur-bar will awaken to a new life in a new body."

It was while I was watching this marvelous operation that a mad plan occurred to me whereby I might eventually reach the side of Janai, or at least discover what fate had overtaken her. I turned to Ras Thavas. "Could you restore Gantun Gur's brain to his head if you wished to?" I asked.

"Certainly."

"Or could you put it in Tor-dur-bar's abandoned skull?"

"Yes."

"How soon after the removal of a brain do you have to replace it with another?"

"The liquid that I pump into the veins and arteries of a body will preserve it indefinitely. The blood I have withdrawn is also preserved similarly. But what are you driving at?"

"I want you to transfer my brain to the body that was Tor-dur-bar's," I said.

"Are you mad?" demanded John Carter.

"No. Well, perhaps a little, if love is madness. As a hormad I can be sent to the Council of the Seven Jeds and perhaps chosen to serve them. I know I can be chosen, for I know what answers to make to their questions. Once there, I can find the opportunity to discover what has become of Janai. Perhaps I may even rescue her, and when I have either succeeded or failed, Ras Thavas can return my brain to my own body. Will you do it, Ras Thavas?"

Ras Thavas looked questioningly at John Carter. "I have no right to interpose any objections," said The Warlord. "Vor Daj's brain and body are his own."

"Very well," said Ras Thavas. "Help me lift the new Tor-dur-bar from the table and then lie down there yourself."

CHAPTER IX

MAN INTO HORMAD

WHEN I REGAINED consciousness, the first sight that met my eyes was that of my own body lying on an ersite slab a few inches from me. It was rather a ghastly experience, looking at one's own corpse; but when I sat up and looked down at my new body, it was even worse. I hadn't anticipated just how horrible it would be to be a hormad with a hideous face and malformed body. I almost loathed to touch myself with my new hands. Suppose something should happen to Ras Thavas! I broke out in a cold sweat at the thought. John Carter and the great surgeon stood looking at me.

"What is the matter?" demanded the latter. "You look ill."

I told him of the fear that had suddenly assailed me. He shrugged. "It would be just too bad for you," he said. "There is another man in the world, probably the only other man in the entire universe, who could restore your brain to your body were anything to happen to me; but you could never get him to Morbus as long as the hormads rule here."

"Who is he?" I asked.

"Vad Varo, a prince of Duhor now. He was Ulysses Paxton of Jasoom, and he was my assistant in my laboratory at Toonol. It was he who transferred my old brain to this new body. But don't worry I have lived over a thousand years. The hormads need me. There is no reason why I should not live another thousand years. Before that I shall have trained another assistant, so that he can transfer my brain to a new body. You see, I should live forever."

"I hope you do," I said. Just then I discovered the body of the assassin of Amhor lying on the floor. "What's the matter with Tor-dur-bar?" I asked. "Shouldn't he have regained consciousness before I did?"

"I saw to it that he didn't," said Ras Thavas. "John Carter and I decided that it might be well if none other than he and I knew that your brain had been transferred to the body of a hormad."

"You were right. Let them think that I am all hormad."

"Carry Tor-dur-bar into my study. Let him come to there, but before he does you must be out of sight. Go out into the laboratory and help with the emergence of the new hormads. Tell the officer there that I sent you."

"But won't Tor-dur-bar recognize me when he sees me later?"

"I think not. He never saw his own face often enough to become familiar with it. There are few mirrors in Morbus, and his new body was such a recent acquisition that there is little likelihood that he will recognize it. If he does, we'll have to tell him."

The next several days were extremely unpleasant. I was a hormad. I had to consort with hormads and eat raw animal tissue. Ras Thavas armed me, and I had to destroy the terrible travesties on humanity that wriggled out of his abominable tanks so malformed that they were useless even as hormads. One day I met Teeaytan-ov, with whom I had flown to Morbus on the back of a malagor. He recognized me, or at least he thought he did.

"Kaor, Tor-dur-bar!" he greeted me. "So you have a new body. What has become of my friend, Vor Daj?"

"I do not know," I said. "Perhaps he went into the vats. He spoke of you often before I lost track of him. He was very anxious that you and I be friends."

"Why not?" asked Teeaytan-ov.

"I think it an excellent idea," I said, for I wanted all the friends I could get. "What are you doing now?"

"I am a member of the Third Jed's bodyguard. I live in the palace."

"That is fine," I said, "and I suppose you see everything that goes on there."

"I see a great deal. It makes me want to be a jed. I should like a new body such as they have."

"I wonder what became of the girl who was brought to the palace at the same time Vor Daj was," I ventured.

"What girl?" he asked.

"She was called Janai."

"Oh, Janai. She is still there. Two of the jeds want her, and the others won't let either have her. At least not so far. They are going to take a vote on it soon. I think every one of them wants her. She is the best looking woman they have captured for a long time."

"She is safe for the time being, then?" I asked.

"What do you mean, safe?" he demanded. "She will be very lucky if one of the jeds acquires her. She will have the best of everything and won't have to go to the vats of Ras Thavas. But why are you so interested in her? Perhaps you want her for yourself," and he burst into laughter. He would have been surprised indeed had he known that he had scored a bull's-eye.

"How do you like being a member of a jed's bodyguard?" I asked.

"It is very fine. I am treated well, have plenty to eat and a nice place to sleep, and I do not have to work hard. Also, I have a great deal of freedom. I can go wherever I please on the island of Morbus except into the private quarters of the jeds. You cannot leave this laboratory." He touched a medal hanging from a chain about his neck. "It is this," he said, "that gives me so much freedom. It shows that I am in the service of the Third Jed. No one dares interfere with me. I am a very important person, Tor-dur-bar. I feel quite sorry for you who are only a piece of animal tissue that can walk around and talk."

"It is nice to have such an important friend as you," I said, "especially one who will help me, if he can."

"Help you in what way?" he asked.

"The jeds are constantly calling for new warriors to replace those that are killed. I would make a good warrior for the bodyguard of a jed, and it would be nice if you and I could be together; so, if I am chosen to appear before them for examination, you can put in a good word for me when they ask who knows me."

He thought this over for a minute in his slow-witted way, but finally he said, "Why not? You look very strong; and sometimes, when the members of the guard get to quarrelling among themselves, it is well to have a strong friend. Yes, I'll help you, if I can. Sometimes they ask us if we know a good strong warrior who is intelligent, and then they send for him and examine him. Of course you are not very intelligent, but you might be able to pass because you are so strong. Just how strong are you?"

As a matter of fact, I didn't know, myself. I knew I was quite strong, because I lifted bodies so easily; so I said, "I really don't know."

"Could you lift me?" he asked. "I am a very heavy person."

"I can try," I said. I picked him up very easily. He didn't seem to weigh anything; so I thought I would see if I could toss him up over my head. I succeeded quite beyond my expectations, or his either. I tossed him almost to the ceiling of the room, and caught him as he came down. As I set him on his feet, he looked at me in astonishment.

"You are the strongest person in Morbus," he said. "There never was any one as strong as you. I shall tell the Third Jed about you."

He went away then, leaving me quite hopeful. At best, I had anticipated that Ras Thavas might some day include me with an assignment of hormads to be examined by the jeds; but as the ranks of the bodyguards were often filled by drafts on the villages outside the city, there was no telling how long I should have to wait for such an opportunity.

Ras Thavas had detailed me as the personal servant of John Carter, so we were not separated; and as he worked constantly with Ras Thavas, the three of us were often together. In the presence of others, they treated me as they would have treated any other hormad—like a dumb and ignorant servant, but when we were alone they accepted me once more as an equal. They both marvelled at my enormous strength, which was merely one of the accidents of the growth of Tor-dur-bar's new body; and I was sure that Ras Thavas would have liked to slice me up and return me to the vats in the hope of producing a new strain of super-powerful hormads.

John Carter is one of the most human persons I have ever known. He is in every sense of the word a great man, a statesman, a soldier, perhaps the greatest swordsman that ever lived, grim and terrible in combat; but with it all he is modest and approachable, and he has never lost his sense of humor. When we were alone he would joke with me about my newly acquired "pulchritude," laughing in his quiet way until his sides shook; and I was, indeed, a sight to inspire both laughter and horror. My great torso on its short legs, my right arm reaching below my knees, my left but slightly below my waist line, I was all out of proportion.

"Your face is really your greatest asset," he said, after looking at me for a long time. "I should like to take you back to Helium as you are and present you at the jeddak's next levee. You know, of course, that you were considered one of the handsomest men in Helium. I should say, 'Here is the noble Vor Daj, a padwar of The Warlord's Guard,' and how the women would cluster around you!"

My face really was something to arrest attention. Not a single feature was placed where it should have been, and all were out of proportion, some being too large and some too small. My right eye was way up on my forehead, just below the hair line, and was twice as large as my left eye which was about half an inch in front of my left ear. My mouth started at the bottom of my chin and ran upward at an angle of about 45° to a point slightly below my huge right eye. My nose was scarcely more than a bud and occupied the place that my little left eye should have had. One ear was close set and tiny, the other a pendulous mass that hung almost to my shoulder. It inclined me to believe that the symmetry of normal humans might not be wholly a matter of accident, as Ras Thavas believed.

Tor-dur-bar, with his new body, had wanted a name instead of a number; so John Carter and Ras Thavas had christened him Tun-gan, a transposition of the syllables of Gantun Gur's first name. When I told them of my conversation with Teeaytan-ov they agreed with me that I should keep the name Tor-dur-bar. Ras Thavas said he would tell Tun-gan that he had grafted a new hormad brain into his old body, and this he did at the first opportunity.

Shortly thereafter I met Tun-gan in one of the laboratory corridors. He looked at me searchingly for a moment, and then stopped me. "What is your name?" he demanded.

"Tor-dur-bar," I replied.

He shuddered visibly. "Are you really as hideous as you appear?" he asked; and then, without waiting for me to reply, "Keep out of my sight if you don't want to go to the incinerator or the vats."

When I told John Carter and Ras Thavas about it, they had a good laugh. It was good to have a laugh occasionally, for there was little here that was amusing. I was worried about Janai as well as the possibility that I might never regain my former body; Ras Thavas was dejected because of the failure of his plan to regain his former laboratory in Toonol and avenge himself on Vobis Kan, the jeddak; and John Carter grieved constantly, I knew, over the fate of his princess.

While we were talking there in Ras Thavas's private study an officer from the palace was announced; and without waiting to be invited, he entered the room. "I have come to fetch the hormad called Tor-dur-bar," he said. "Send for him without delay."

"This is an order from the Council of the Seven Jeds," said the officer. He was a sullen, arrogant fellow; doubtless one of the red captives into whose skull the brain of a hormad had been grafted.

Ras Thavas shrugged and pointed at me. "This is Tor-dur-bar," he said.

CHAPTER X

I FIND JANAI

SEVEN OTHER HORMADS were lined up with me before the dais on which sat the seven jeds. I was, perhaps, the ugliest of them all. They asked us many questions. It was, in a way, a crude intelligence test, for they wished hormads above the average in intelligence to serve in this select body of monstrous guardsmen. I was to learn that they were becoming a little appearance conscious, also; for one of the jeds looked long at me, and then waved me aside.

"We do not want such a hideous creature in the guards," he said.

I looked around at the other hormads in the chamber, and really couldn't see much to choose from between them and me. They were all hideous monsters. What difference could it make that I was a little more hideous? Of course there was nothing for me to do; and, much disappointed, I stepped back from the line.

Five of the seven remaining were little better than half-wits, and they were eliminated. The other two might have been high grade morons at the best, but they were accepted. The Third Jed spoke to an officer. "Where is the hormad I sent for?" he demanded. "Tor-dur-bar."

"I am Tor-dur-bar," I said.

"Come here," said the Third Jed, and again I stepped to the foot of the dais.

"One of my guardsmen says you are the strongest person in Morbus," continued the Third Jed. "Are you?"

"I don't know," I replied. "I am very strong."

"He says that you can toss a man to the ceiling and catch him again. Let me see you do it."

I picked up one of the rejected hormads and threw him as high as I could. I learned then that I didn't know my own strength. The room was quite lofty, but the creature hit the ceiling with a dull thud and fell back into my arms unconscious. The seven jeds and the others in the room looked at me with astonishment.

"He may not be beautiful," said the Third Jed, "but I shall take him for my guard."

The jed who had waved me aside objected. "Guardsmen must be intelligent," he said. "This creature looks as though it had no brains at all."

"We shall see," said another jed, and then they commenced to fire questions at me. Of course they were simple questions that the most ignorant of red men could have answered easily, for the questioners had only the brains and experience of hormads after all.

"He is very intelligent," said the Third Jed. "He answers all our questions easily. I insist upon having him."

"We shall draw lots for him," said the First Jed.

"We shall do nothing of the kind," stormed the Third Jed. "He belongs to me. It was I who sent for him. None of the rest of you had ever heard of him."

"We shall take a vote on it," said the Fourth Jed.

The Fifth Jed, who had rejected me, said nothing. He just sat there scowling. I had made a fool of him by proving myself so desirable that many jeds wished me.

"Come," said the Seventh Jed, "let's take a vote to see whether we award him to the Third Jed or draw lots for him."

"Don't waste time," said the Third Jed, "for I am going to take him anyway." He was a big man, larger than any of his fellows.

"You are always making trouble," growled the First Jed.

"It is the rest of you that are making trouble," retorted the Third Jed, "by trying to deprive me of what is rightfully mine."

"The Third Jed is right," said the Second Jed. "None of the rest of us have any claim on this hormad. We were willing to see him rejected until the Third Jed proved that he would make a desirable guardsman."

They wrangled on for a long time, but finally gave in to the Third Jed. Now I had a new master. He put me in charge of one of his own officers and I was taken away to be initiated into the duties of a guardsman in the palace of the seven jeds of Morbus.

The officer conducted me to a large guardroom where there were many other hormad warriors. Teeaytan-ov was among them, and he lost no time in claiming credit for having me chosen for the guards. One of the first things I was taught was that I was to fight and die, if necessary, in defense of the Third Jed. I was given the insignia of the guard to wear around my neck, and then an officer undertook to train me in the use of a longsword. I had to pretend to a little awkwardness lest he discover that I was more familiar with the weapon than he. He complimented me upon my aptitude, and said that he would give me daily instruction thereafter.

I found my fellow guardsmen a stupid, egotistical lot of morons. They were all jealous of one another and of the seven jeds who were only hormads after all with the bodies of red men. I discovered that only fear held them in leash, for they were just intelligent enough to resent their lot and to envy the officers and jeds who had power and authority. The soil was ripe for mutiny or revolution. It was just an undercurrent that one sensed if he had intelligence, for they feared spies and informers too much to voice their true feeling aloud.

I chafed now at every delay that kept me from searching for Janai. I did not dare make any inquiries concerning her, as that would immediately have aroused suspicion; nor did I dare go poking about the palace until I knew more of its customs and its life.

The following day I was taken with a detachment of guardsmen beyond the walls of the city out among the crowded villages of the common hormads. Here I saw thousands of monstrous creatures, stupid and sullen, with no pleasures beyond eating and sleeping, and just enough intelligence ordinarily to make them dissatisfied with their lot. There were many, of course, with less brains and no more imagination than beasts. These alone were contented.

I saw envy and hate in the glances that many of them cast upon us and our officers, and there were growling murmurs after we had passed that followed us like the low moaning of the wind in the wake of a flier. I came to the conclusion that the Seven Jeds of Morbus were going to find many obstacles in the way of their grandiose plan to conquer a world with these creatures, and the most insurmountable of all would be the creatures themselves.

At last I learned the ways of the palace and how to find my way about, and the first time I was off duty I commenced a systematic search for Janai. I always moved quickly, as though I was on some important errand; so when I met officers or hormads they paid no attention to me.

One day, as I came to the end of a corridor, a hormad stepped from the doorway and confronted me. "What are you doing here?" he demanded. "Don't you know that these are the quarters of the women and that no one is allowed here except those who guard them?"

"You are one of the guards?" I asked.

"Yes; now be on your way, and don't come back here again."

"It must be a very important post, guarding the women," I said.

He swelled perceptibly. "It is, indeed. Only the most trustworthy warriors are chosen."

"Are the women very beautiful?" I asked.

"Very," he said.

"I certainly envy you. I wish that I might be a guard here, too. It would make me happy to see these beautiful women. I have never seen one. Just to get a glimpse of them would be wonderful."

"Well," he said, "perhaps it would do no harm to let

you have a little glimpse. You seem to be a very intelligent fellow. What is your name?"

"I am Tor-dur-bar," I said. "I am in the guard of the Third Jed."

"You are Tor-dur-bar, the strongest man in Morbus?" he demanded.

"Yes, I am he."

"I have heard of you. Every one is talking about you, and how you threw a hormad up against the ceiling of the council chamber so hard that you killed him. I shall be very glad to let you have a look at the women, but don't tell anybody that I did so."

"Of course not," I assured him.

He stepped to the door at the end of the corridor and swung it open. Beyond was a large chamber in which were several women and a number of the sexless hormads who were evidently their servants.

"You may step in," said the guard; "they will think you are another guard."

I entered the room and looked quickly about, and as I did so my heart leaped to my throat, for there, at the far end of the room, was Janai. Forgetful of everything else, I started to cross toward her. I forgot the guard. I forgot that I was a hideous monster. I forgot everything but that here was the woman I loved and here was I. The guard overtook me and laid a hand upon my shoulder.

"Hey! Where are you going?" he demanded.

Then I came to myself. "I wanted to get a closer look at them," I said. "I wanted to see what it was that the jeds saw in women."

"Well, you have seen enough. I don't see what they see in them, myself. Come now, you must get out."

As he spoke the door by which we had entered swung open again, and the Third Jed entered. The guard shrivelled in terror. "Quick!" he gasped. "Mingle with the servants. Pretend you are one of them. Perhaps he will not notice you."

I crossed quickly toward Janai and kneeled before her. "What do you want?" she demanded. "What are you doing here, hormad? You are not one of our servants."

"I have a message for you," I whispered. I touched her with my hand. I could not help it. I could scarcely resist the tremendous urge I felt to take her in my arms. She shrank from me, an expression of loathing and disgust upon her face.

"Do not touch me, hormad," she said, "or I shall call the guard."

Then I remembered the hideous monster that I was, and I drew away from her. "Do not call the guard until you have heard my message," I begged.

"There is no one here to send me any message I would care to hear," she said.

"There is Vor Daj," I said. "Have you forgotten him?" I waited breathlessly to note her reaction.

"Vor Daj!" she breathed in a whisper. "He has sent you to me?"

"Yes. He told me to find you. He did not know but that you were dead. He told me that if I found you I was to tell you that day and night he was searching for some plan whereby he might take you away from Morbus."

"There can be no hope," she said, "but tell him that I have not forgotten him and never shall. Every day I think of him, and now every day I shall bless him for thinking of me and wishing to help me."

I was about to say more to her, to tell her that Vor Daj loved her, so that I might see whether that pleased her or not; but then I heard a loud voice demand, "What are you doing here?" and turning I saw that the First Jed had entered the room and was confronting the Third Jed accusingly.

"I have come after my slave woman," replied the latter. "What are you going to do about it?"

"These women have not been distributed by the Council. You have no right to any of them. If you need more slaves, order some additional hormads. Come on, get out of here!"

For answer, the Third Jed crossed the room and seized Janai by one arm. "Come with me, woman," he ordered, and started to drag her toward the door; then the First Jed whipped out his sword and blocked the way. The sword of the Third Jed flashed from its scabbard, and the two men engaged, which necessitated the Third Jed's relinquishing his hold on Janai.

The duel was a rare spectacle of poor swordsmanship, but they skipped about the room so much and cut and slashed so terrifically in all directions that the other occupants of the chamber had to keep constantly on the move to avoid injury. I tried always to keep between them and Janai, and presently I found myself near the door with the girl close beside me. The attention of the guard as well as all others in the room was riveted upon the two combatants, and the door was just behind us. Nowhere could Janai be in greater danger than here. Perhaps never again would I have such an opportunity to get her out of these quarters in which she was a prisoner. Where I could take her, I did not know; but to get her out of here would be something. If, in some way, I could smuggle her into the laboratory I was sure that John Carter and Ras Thavas would find some place to hide her Bending my ugly face close to her beautiful one, I whispered, "Come with me," but she shrank away. "Please don't be afraid of me," I begged. "I am doing this for Vor Daj, because he is my friend. I want to try to help you."

"Very well," she said, without further hesitation.

I looked hurriedly about the room. No one was paying any attention to us. Every eye was centered upon the combatants. I took Janai's hand, and together we slipped through the doorway out into the corridor beyond.

CHAPTER XI

WAR OF THE SEVEN JEDS

NOW THAT WE were out of the room where Janai had been imprisoned I hadn't the slightest idea where to take her. The suspicions of the first person who saw us together would be aroused. I asked Janai if she knew any place where I might hide her safely until I could find a way to get her out of the palace. She said that she did not. She knew only the room in which she had been imprisoned.

I hurried her down the corridor along which I had come, but at the head of the ramp leading to the floor below I saw two officers ascending. There was a door at my left; and as we had to get out of sight immediately, I opened it and hurried Janai into the room beyond, which, fortunately, was vacant. It was evidently a storeroom, for there were sacks and boxes piled along the walls. At the far end of the room was a window, and in one of the side walls another door.

I waited until I heard the officers pass along the corridor; then I opened the door in the side wall to see what lay beyond. There was another room in one corner of which was a pile of sleeping silks and furs. Everything was covered with dust, indicating that the room had not been occupied for a considerable time. In a curtained alcove was a bath, and from hooks along the wall hung the trappings of a warrior, even to his weapons. The former occupant must have left, expecting to return; and my guess was that he had been an officer who had gone out on some expedition and been killed, for the trappings and weapons that had been left behind were such as a fighting man wears upon dress occasions.

"We have stumbled upon an excellent place for you to hide," I said. "Keep the door to this room locked: there is a bolt on this side. I shall bring you food when I can, and just as soon as it is possible I'll get you to a safer place."

"Perhaps Vor Daj will come to see me," she suggested. "Be sure to tell him where I am."

"He would come if he could; but he is in the laboratory building, and cannot get out. Would you like to see him very much?" I couldn't resist asking her that.

"Very much, indeed," she said.

"He will be glad to know that, and until he can come I'll do the best I can to help you."

"Why are you so kind to me?" she asked. "You seem very different from the other hormads I have seen."

"I am Vor Daj's friend," I said. "I will do anything I can for him and for you. You are no longer afraid of me?"

"No. I was at first, but not now."

"You need never be afraid of me. There is nothing that I would not do for you, even to laying down my life for you."

"I thank you, even though I do not understand," she said.

"Some day you will understand, but not yet. Now I must be going. Be brave, and don't give up hope."

"Goodbye,—Oh, I do not even know your name."

"I am called Tor-dur-bar," I said.

"Oh, now I remember you. Your head was cut off in the fight in which Vor Daj and Dotar Sojat were captured. I remember that then you promised to be Vor Daj's friend. Now you have a new body."

"I wish they might have given me a new face as well," I said, simulating a smile with my hideous great mouth.

"It is enough that you have a good heart," she said.

"It is enough for me that you think so, Janai; and now goodbye."

As I passed through the outer room I examined the sacks and boxes piled there, and was overjoyed to discover that they contained food. I hastened to acquaint Janai with this good news; then I left her and returned to the guard-room.

My fellow guardsmen were most uninteresting companions. Like most stupid people they talked principally about themselves and were great braggarts. Food was also a very important topic of conversation with them, and they would spend hours telling of the great quantities of animal tissue they had eaten upon various occasions. When there was no officer around they aired their grievances against the authority of the jeds; but this they did fearfully, as there was always the danger of spies or informers. Promotions to easier berths and larger allowances of animal tissue were the rewards for informing on one's fellows.

I had been back but a short time when an officer entered the room and ordered us to strap on our weapons and accompany him. He marched us to a very large room in the quarters of the Third Jed, to whom we belonged; and there I found that all the armed retainers of the jed were gathered. There was much whispering and speculation. The officers appeared unusually serious, and the atmosphere seemed charged with nervous apprehension.

Presently the Third Jed entered the room accompanied by his four principal dwars He had been bleeding from several wounds which had been bandaged. I knew where he had acquired them, and I wondered how the First Jed had fared. The Third Jed mounted a dais and addressed us.

"You will accompany me to the Council of the Seven Jeds," he said. "It is your duty to see that no harm befalls me. Obey your officers. If you are loyal, you will receive an extra allowance of food and many privileges. I have spoken."

We were marched to the council chamber which was jammed with the armed hormads of the personal bodyguards of the seven jeds. The air was tense with suppressed excitement. Even the stupidest hormads seemed infected by it. Six jeds sat upon the dais. The First Jed was swathed in bandages that were red with blood. The throne of the Third Jed was empty. Surrounding our jed, we shouldered our way to the foot of the dais; but he did not mount to the throne. Instead, he stood on the floor facing the six jeds; and his voice and his manner were truculent as he addressed them.

"You sent warriors to arrest me," he said. "They are dead. There is no one in Morbus with the power or authority to arrest me. There are some among you who would like to be jeddak and rule the rest of us. The First Jed would like to be jeddak. The time has come for us to determine which one is fit to be jeddak, for I agree with others of you that seven men cannot rule as well as one. Divided authority is no authority."

"You are under arrest," shouted the First Jed.

The Third Jed laughed at him. "You are giving additional proof that you are not fit to be jeddak, for you can only issue orders—you cannot enforce them."

The First Jed looked down at his followers, addressing his chief dwar. "Seize him!" he commanded. "Take the traitor dead or alive."

The warriors of the First Jed moved toward us, forcing their way slowly through crowds of other warriors. I chanced to be standing in the front row, facing the oncoming hormads. A big warrior was the first to shoulder his way through to us. He made a pass at me with his sword. He was very slow and clumsy, and I had no difficulty stepping quickly to one side and avoiding it. He had put so much into that blow, that, when he missed me, he lost his balance and came tumbling into my arms. That was wonderful! I hoisted him in to the air and threw him fully fifty feet from me, so that he alighted in the midst of his companions, knocking many of them to the floor.

"Good work, Tor-dur-bar!" shouted the Third Jed. "You shall have all the meat you want for that."

A second man reached me and I threw him all the way across the room. I was just beginning to appreciate what enormous strength I had. It seemed absolutely incredible that any creature could be so strong. After that there was a lull during which the Third Jed succeeded in making himself heard again.

"I, the Third Jed," he thundered, "now proclaim myself Jeddak of Morbus. Let the jeds who will swear allegiance to me rise!"

No one rose. It looked bad for the Third Jed, as the chamber was packed with the warriors of the other jeds. It also looked pretty bad for us. I wondered what the Third Jed would do. It seemed to me that his life was forfeit anyway, no matter what he did. He turned and spoke to the dwars clustered about him, and immediately orders were given for us to fall back to the doorway. Then the fighting began as the other jeds ordered their warriors to prevent our escape.

The Third Jed called me by name. "Clear a way to the door, Tor-dur-bar!" he cried. It seemed to me that he was banking rather too heavily upon my strength; but I enjoyed fighting, and this looked like an excellent opportunity to get my fill of it. I forced my way back through our own ranks to what was now the front rank of our attack, and here I found that fate had given me a great advantage in one of my deformities. My enormously long arm was my sword arm, which, backed by my super-human strength and a long sword, permitted me to cut a swath through the enemy line that opened a path as by magic, for those that I did not mow down turned and fled before the intensity of my attack.

There were heads and arms and legs and halves of bodies writhing and squirming on the floor; there were heads screaming and cursing under foot, and headless bodies dashing about the room colliding with friend and foe indiscriminately. If there ever was a shambles it was there in the great council chamber of the seven jeds of Morbus. The hormads were, for the most part, too stupid to know fear; but when they saw their officers fleeing from me, their morale was shattered; and we won to the door with scarcely a casualty on our side.

From there our officers led us out of the palace into the city and down the long avenue to the city gates. There they knew nothing of what had been going on in the palace, and swung the gates open at the command of the Third Jed. Of course, they couldn't have stopped us anyway, for we greatly outnumbered the guard at the gates.

I wondered where we were going as we marched out of the city of Morbus; but I was soon to discover, for at the first of the outer villages that we came to, the Third Jed demanded its surrender, and announced that he was the Jeddak of Morbus. He swore the officers and warriors into his service, promoted many of the former, promised increased rations to the latter, left a dwar to represent him and marched on to new conquests.

Nowhere did he meet with opposition, and in three days he had conquered all of the island of Morbus except the city itself. The dwars he left behind organized the local warriors to oppose any force that might be sent out by the six jeds remaining in command of the city, but during those three days no army marched out of Morbus to contest the right of the new jeddak to rule.

On the fifth day we marched back to a large village on

the coast, near the city; and here Aymad, Jeddak of Morbus, established his capital. This is the name he took, the literal translation of which is One-man, or Number One Man, or First Man. Anyway, he was head man; and I think that of all the seven jeds he was best fitted to be jeddak. He had a physique and face suited to his new role, and he possessed one of the best brains of any of the hormads that I had knowledge of.

Of course all that had happened seemed at the time to have placed me in an utterly hopeless position. Janai was in the city beyond any hope of my succoring her I was separated from The Warlord and from Ras Thavas. I was only a poor hormad without influence or position I could do nothing, and by now I must have been so well known in the city that I could not possibly enter it surreptitiously My hideous features must by this time have become all too well known to the followers of the six jeds to permit me the slightest hope of entering the city unrecognized.

When we finally encamped in the new capital of Ay-mad I threw myself upon the ground with my fellow hormads and awaited the issuance of the slimy animal tissue that was our principal reward for the conquests we had made It satisfied most of the poor, moronic, half-witted creatures who were my comrades; but it did not satisfy me. I was endowed with more brains, more ability, more experience, more physical strength than any of them. I was by far a better man than the jeddak himself; and yet I was only a hideous, malformed hormad that no self-respecting calot would associate with. I was thus occupied with self-pity when an officer came calling my name aloud. I stood up.

"I am Tor-dur-bar," I said.

"Come with me," he said. "The Jeddak has sent for you"

I accompanied him to where the Jeddak and all his principal officers were gathered, wondering what new task Ay-mad had conceived for the testing of my enormous strength, for I could not believe that he wished to see me for any other purpose. I had acquired the typical inferiority of a true hormad.

They had fixed up a sort of a dais and throne for Ay-mad, and he sat there like a regular jeddak with his officers grouped around him. "Approach, Tor-dur-bar!" he commanded, and so I came forward and stood before the throne. "Kneel," he said, and I kneeled, for I was only a poor hormad. "More than to any other the victory that we won in the council chamber in Morbus was due to you."

he said. "You not only have the strength of many men, but you have intelligence. Because of these things I appoint you a dwar, and when we enter Morbus in victory you may select the body of any red man there and I will command Ras Thavas to transfer your brain to it."

So I was a dwar. I thanked Ay-mad, and joined the other dwars clustered about him. They all had the bodies of red men. How many of them had hormad brains, I did not know. I was the only dwar with the body of a hormad. I might, as far as I knew, be the only one with the brains of a human being.

CHAPTER XII

WARRIOR'S REWARD

MORBUS IS A walled city. It is practically impregnable to men armed only with swords. For seven days Ay-mad tried to take it, but all his warriors could do was to beat futilely upon the great wooden gates while the defending warriors dropped heavy stones on their heads. At night we withdrew, and the defenders probably went to sleep with a sense of perfect security. On the eighth day Ay-mad called a conference of his dwars. "We are getting nowhere," he said. "We could pound on those gates for a thousand years and do nothing more important than make dents in them. How are we to take Morbus? If we conquer the world we must capture Morbus and Ras Thavas."

"You cannot conquer the world," I said, "but you can take Morbus."

"Why can't we conquer the world?" he demanded.

"It is too large, and there are too many great nations to be overcome."

"What do you know about the world?" he demanded. "You are only a hormad who has never been outside of Morbus."

"You will see that I am right, if you try to conquer the world; but it would be easy to take the city of Morbus."

"And how?" he asked.

I told him in a few words how I should do it were I in command. He looked at me for a long time, thinking the matter out. "It is too simple," he said; then he turned on the others. "Why have none of you thought of this before?" he demanded. "Tor-dur-bar is the only man of brains among you."

All that night a thousand hormads were engaged in building long ladders, all that night and the next day. We had a thousand of them, and when both moons had passed below the horizon on the second night a hundred thousand hormads crept toward the walls of Morbus with their long ladders. In a thousand places all around the city we raised our ladders to the top of the walls, and at a given signal a hundred men scaled each ladder and dropped into the city streets.

The rest was easy. We took the sleeping city with the loss of only a few warriors; and Ay-mad, with his dwars, entered the council chamber. The first thing that he did was to have all but one throne removed from the dais; then, seated there, he had the six jeds dragged before him. They were a sheepish, terrified lot.

"How do you wish to die?" he asked, "or would you rather have your brains returned to the skulls of hormads from whence they came?"

"That cannot be done," said the Fifth Jed, "but if it could, I would rather go to the vats. I do not wish to be a hormad again."

"Why can't it be done?" demanded Ay-mad. "What Ras Thavas has done so many times, he can do again."

"There is no Ras Thavas," said the Fifth Jed. "He has disappeared."

The effect that that statement had upon me may well be imagined. If it were true, I was doomed to lifetime imprisonment in the monstrous carcass of a hormad. There could be no escape, for Vad Varo of Duhor was as far removed from me as though he had been back upon his own planet of Jasoom; and he was the only other man in the world who could restore my brain to its rightful body if Ras Thavas were dead. With the new Jeddak of Morbus seeking to conquer the world, all men would be our enemies. I could not call upon any man to save me.

And what of Janai? I should always be repulsive to her, and so I could never tell her the truth. It were far better that she believe me dead than that she should know that my brain was forever buried behind this loathsome, inhuman mask. How could one with an exterior like mine speak of love? And love was not for hormads.

In a daze, I heard Ay-mad ask what had become of Ras Thavas and the Fifth Jed reply, "No one knows. He has simply disappeared. As he could not escape from the city

60

without detection, we believe that some of the hormads sliced him up and threw him into one of his own culture vats in revenge."

Ay-mad was furious, for without Ras Thavas his dream of world conquest was shattered. "This is the work of my enemies," he cried. "Some of you six jeds had a hand in this. You have destroyed Ras Thavas or hidden him. Take them away! Put them in separate dungeons in the pits. The one who confesses first shall have his life and his liberty. The rest shall die. I give you one day to decide."

After the six jeds had been dragged away Ay-mad offered amnesty to all of their officers who would swear allegiance to him, an invitation which was refused by none, since refusal could mean nothing but death. After this formality, which took a matter of some hours, was completed, Ay-mad publicly acknowledged that the success of his operations against Morbus was due to me; and told me that he would grant me any favor that I might ask and that in addition to that he was appointing me an odwar, a military rank analogous to that of general in the armies of the planet Earth.

"And now," continued Ay-mad, "choose the favor that you would ask."

"That I should like to do in private," I said, "for the favor I wish to ask can be of no interest to any but you and me."

"Very well," he said. "I grant you a private audience immediately upon the conclusion of this one."

It was with some impatience that I awaited the conclusion of the session in the council chamber, and when at last Ay-mad arose and motioned me to follow him I breathed a sigh of relief. He led me into a small apartment directly behind the dais and seated himself behind a large desk.

"Now," he said, "what is the favor you wish to ask?"

"I am going to ask two," I replied. "I should like to be placed in full charge of the laboratory building."

"I see no objection to that," he interrupted. "But why such a strange request?"

"There is the body of a red man there to which I should like to have my brain transferred if Ras Thavas is ever found," I explained, "and if I am in full charge of the laboratory building I can protect the body and make sure that Ras Thavas performs the operation."

"Very well," he said, "your request is granted. What is the other?"

"I want you to give me the girl, Janai."

61

His face clouded at that. "What do you want of a girl?" he demanded. "You are only a hormad."

"Some day I may be a red man."

"But why the girl, Janai? What do you know of her? I didn't know you had ever seen her."

"I was with the party that captured her. She is the only woman I have ever seen that I wanted."

"I couldn't give her to you if I had a mind to," he said. "She, too, has disappeared. While I was fighting with the First Jed she must have escaped from the room—we were fighting in the apartment in which the women were being held—and she has not been seen since."

"Will you give her to me if she is found?"

"I want her myself."

"But you have the pick of many others. I have seen beautiful women in the palace; and among them there must be one who would make you a splendid wife, a suitable consort for a jeddak. This, of all the favors I might ask, I wish the most."

"She would rather die than belong to a hideous monster like you," he said.

"Well, grant me this, then: that if she is found the decision be left to her."

He laughed. "That I agree to willingly. You don't think, do you, that she would choose you in preference to a jeddak, a monster in preference to a man?"

"I have been told that women are unpredictable. I am willing to take the chance and abide by her decision, if you are."

"Then it is agreed," he said, and he was quite good natured about it, so certain was he of the outcome; "but you are not getting much in the way of reward for the services you have rendered me. I thought you would at least ask for a palace of your own and many servants."

"I asked for the two things I wish most," I said, "and I am content."

"Well, you may have the palace and the servants whenever you wish them, for by your own proposition you will never have the girl, even if she be found."

As soon as he dismissed me I hurried to the apartment where I had left Janai, and my heart was in my mouth for fear that I should not find her there. I had to be careful that no one saw me enter the storeroom that led to her hiding place, for I did not want Ay-mad ever to discover that I had known all along where she was hidden. Fortunately the corridor was empty, and I entered the storeroom unseen. Going to the door of Janai's room, I knocked. There was no answer.

"Janai!" I called. "It is I, Tor-dur-bar. Are you there?"

Then I heard the bolt being withdrawn, and the door swung open. There she stood! My heart almost stopped for very relief. And she was so beautiful! It seemed that each new time I saw her she had become more beautiful.

"You are back," she said. "I began to fear that you would never come. Do you bring word from Vor Daj?"

So she was thinking of Vor Daj! On such slight sustenance does love thrive. I entered the room and closed the door.

"Vor Daj sends greetings," I said. "He thinks of nothing but you and your welfare."

"But he cannot come to me?"

"No. He is a prisoner in the laboratory building, but he has charged me to look after you. Now I can do so better than before for many changes have taken place in Morbus since I last saw you. I am an odwar now, and my influence with the new jeddak is considerable."

"I have been hearing sounds of fighting," she said. "Tell me what has happened."

I told her briefly and that the Third Jed was now jeddak. "Then I am lost," she said, "for he is all powerful."

"Perhaps that is your salvation," I told her. "To reward me for the services I had rendered him, the new jeddak made me an odwar and promised to grant me any favor I asked."

"And what did you ask of him?"

"You."

I could almost feel the shudder that ran through her frame as she looked at my hideous face and deformed body. "Please!" she begged. "You said you were my friend, that you were the friend of Vor Daj. He would not wish you to have me, I am sure."

"I only asked for you that I might protect you for Vor Daj," I said.

"How does Vor Daj know that I would have him?" she demanded.

"He doesn't know. He only hopes that I may protect you from others. I have not said, have I, that Vor Daj wishes you for himself?" I could not resist saying that just to match her seeming indifference to Vor Daj. Her chin went up a little, and that pleased me. I know something of women and their reactions.

"What did the Third Jed say when you asked for me?" she inquired.

63

"He is jeddak now, and he calls himself Ay-mad," I explained. "He said that you would not have me; so I have come to lay the whole matter before you. It is for you to decide. I think that Vor Daj loves you. You must choose between him and Ay-mad. Ay-mad will ask you to make the choice between him and me; but the choice will really be between him and Vor Daj, only Ay-mad won't know that. If you choose me, Ay-mad will be insulted and angry; but I believe that he will keep his bargain. Then I shall take you to quarters near my own and protect you until such time as you and Vor Daj can escape from Morbus. I can also assure you that Vor Daj will hold you to no promise afterward. His only thought now is to help you."

"I was sure that he would be like that," she said, "and you may be sure that when the choice is given me I shall choose you rather than Ay-mad."

"Even though by choosing him you could become a jeddara?" I asked.

"Even so," she said.

CHAPTER XIII

JOHN CARTER DISAPPEARS

AFTER LEAVING JANAI I went at once to the laboratory building to find John Carter and learn what he knew of the disappearance of Ras Thavas. Janai and I had decided that she should remain where she was for a few days so that Ay-mad's suspicions would not be aroused by my finding her too easily. I had determined to institute a search during which she should be found by someone else, though I would be close at hand to prevent any miscarriage of our plans.

One of the first persons I met on entering the laboratory building was Tun Gan. At sight of me he flew into a rage. "I thought I told you to keep out of my sight," he blustered. "Do you want to go to the incinerator?"

I pointed to my badge of office, which he evidently had not noticed. "You wouldn't send one of the jeddak's odwars to the incinerator, would you?" I inquired.

He was dumfounded. "You an odwar?" he demanded.

"Why not?" I asked.

"But you are only a hormad."

"Perhaps, but I am also an odwar. I could have you sent

to the incinerator or the vats, but I don't intend to. I have your body; so we should be friends. What do you say?"

"All right," he agreed. What else could he do? "But I don't understand how you got to be an odwar with that awful looking face and your deformed body."

"Don't forget that they were your face and body once," I reminded him. "And also don't forget that you couldn't get anywhere with them. It takes more than a face or body to get places—it takes a brain that is good for something beside thinking of food."

"I still can't understand why you should be made an odwar when there are such fine looking men as I to choose from."

"Well, never mind. That isn't what I came here to discuss. I have been placed in full charge of the laboratory building. I have come to talk with John Carter. Do you know where he is?"

"No. Neither does any one else. He disappeared at the same time Ras Thavas did."

That was a new blow. John Carter gone! But on second thought the fact gave me renewed hope. If they were both gone and nobody knew what had become of them, it seemed to me quite possible that they had found the means to escape together. I was certain John Carter would never desert me. If he were gone of his own free will, he would return. He'd never leave me housed in this awful carcass.

"Has no one any idea of what became of them?" I asked.

"They may have been sliced up and thrown into one of the vats," said Tun Gan. "Some of the older hormads have been getting out of hand, and Ras Thavas had threatened them with the incinerator. They might have done it to save themselves or just to be revenged upon him."

"I'm going to Ras Thavas's study," I said. "Come with me."

I found the study in about the same condition I had last seen it. There was nothing to indicate that a struggle of any kind had taken place, not a clue that pointed to any solution of the mystery. I was completely baffled.

"When were they last seen?"

"About three days ago. One of the hormads said he saw them coming up from the pits. I don't know why they were there. No one goes there any more since they stopped storing bodies, and no prisoners are kept there. They use the pits beneath some of the other buildings for them."

"Were the pits searched?"

"Yes, but no trace of them was found."

"Wait here a minute," I said. I wanted to go into the small laboratory and have a look at my body. I wanted to be sure it was safe, but I didn't wish Tun Gan to see it I had an idea that he would suspect something if he saw my body. He wasn't very brilliant, but it wouldn't have taken much intelligence to guess what had become of the brain of Vor Daj.

Tun Gan waited for me in the study. I knew where the key to the small laboratory was hidden, because Ras Thavas had shown me; and I was soon turning it in the lock. A moment later I stepped into the room, and then I got another shock—*my body had disappeared!*

My knees became so weak that I collapsed onto a bench, and there I sat with my head in my hands. My body gone! With it had gone my last hope of winning Janai. It was unthinkable that I could win her with this awful face and grotesque body. I wouldn't have wanted to win her like that. I couldn't have had any respect for her or for any other woman who could have chosen such an abominable creature as I.

Presently I gathered myself together and walked over to the table where I had last seen my body. Everything seemed to be in order, except that the container that had held my blood was missing. Could it be possible that Ras Thavas had transferred another brain to my body? He couldn't have done it without John Carter's approval, and if John Carter had approved there must have been a good reason for it. One occurred to me. They might have found an opportunity to escape from the island that had to be taken advantage of on the instant or not at all. In that case, it might have seemed wiser to John Carter to have another brain transferred to my skull and take my body along with him, rather than leave it here in danger of destruction. Of course he would only have done this had he been assured that they could return later and rescue me. But of course this was all idle conjecture. The truth of the matter was that there was no explanation.

As I sat there thinking about the matter, I recalled the case history that Ras Thavas had written and hung at the foot of the table where my body lay. I thought I would take a look at it and see if any further entries had been made, but when I walked to the foot of the table I saw that the history was not there. In its place hung a single sheet on which were written two numbers—"3–17." What did they signify? Nothing, as far as I was concerned.

I returned to the study and directed Tun Gan to accompany me while I made an inspection of the laboratories, for if I were to be in charge I'd have to make some semblance of a gesture in line with my newly acquired authority.

"How have things been going since Ras Thavas disappeared?" I asked Tun Gan.

"Not so well," he replied. "In fact things seem to go all wrong without him," and when I reached the first vat room I realized that that was a crass understatement of fact. Things couldn't well have been much worse. The floor was covered with the remains of hideous monstrosities that the officers had had to have destroyed. The parts still lived. Legs were trying to walk, hands were clutching at whatever came within reach, heads were lying about screaming and moaning. I called the officer in charge to me.

"What is the meaning of this?" I demanded. "Why hasn't something been done with these things?"

"Who are you to question me, hormad?" he demanded.

I touched the insignia of my rank, and his attitude changed sharply. "I am in charge here now," I said. "Answer my questions."

"No one but Ras Thavas knew exactly how to slice them up for the vats," he said, "nor which vats to put them in."

"Have them taken to the incinerator," I said. "Until Ras Thavas returns burn all that are useless."

"Something has gone wrong in No. 4 vat room," he said. "Perhaps you had better have a look in there."

When I reached No. 4 the sight that met my eyes was one of the most horrible I have ever looked upon. Something had evidently gone wrong with the culture medium, and instead of individual hormads being formed, there was a single huge mass of animal tissue emerging from the vat and rolling out over the floor. Various internal and external human parts and organs grew out of it without any relation to other parts, a leg here, a hand there, a head somewhere else; and the heads were mouthing and screaming, which only added to the horror of the scene.

"We tried to do something about it," said the officer, "but when we tried to kill the mess, the hands clutched us and the heads bit us. Even our hormads were afraid to go near it, and if anything is too horrible for them you can't expect human beings to stomach it."

I quite agreed with him. Frankly, I didn't know what to do. I couldn't get near the vat to drain off the culture medium and stop the growth; and with the hormads afraid to approach it, it would be impossible to destroy it.

"Shut the doors and windows," I said. "Eventually it will smother itself or starve to death," but as I was leaving the room I saw one of the heads take a large bite from an adjacent piece of the tissue. At least it wouldn't starve to death.

The scene haunted me for a long time afterward, and I couldn't rid my mind of speculation upon what was transpiring in that chamber of horrors, behind those closed doors and windows.

I spent several days trying to get things straightened out in the laboratory building; and succeeded, largely due to the fact that no one knew just how to prepare the tissue for the culture vats as they were emptied by the development of their horrid spawn. The result was a rapidly decreasing output of hormads, for which I was, of course, thankful. Soon there would be no more of them, and I could have wished that Ras Thavas might never return to renew his obscene labors had it not been for the fact that only through him might I hope to reclaim my own body.

During this time I did not visit Janai, lest her hiding place be discovered and Ay-mad suspicious that he had been tricked; but at last I determined that it would be safe to "find" her; and so I went to Ay-mad, told him that I had been unsuccessful in locating her, and that I was about to institute a thorough search of the palace.

"If you find her," he said, "you will find only a corpse. She could not have left the palace. I think you will agree with me there, for no woman could leave this palace without being seen by a member of the guard or one of our spies."

"But what makes you think her dead?" I asked.

"People cannot live without food or drink, and I have had you and everyone else who might have taken food to her watched. No food has been taken to her. Go on with your search, Tor-dur-bar. Your reward, if there is reward at all, will be the body of a dead woman."

There was something in his expression when he said this that gave me pause. That half smile of his—cunning and self-satisfied. What did it denote? Had he found Janai and had her destroyed? Immediately I began to worry. I conjured all sorts of horrible pictures, and it was with the greatest difficulty that I restrained myself from going at once to Janai's hiding place that I might learn the truth. But my better judgment prevailed; and, instead, I immediately organized a searching party. I put trustworthy officers in charge; and directed each to search a given part of the palace, looking in every room, closet, cubby hole. I accompanied one of the parties. This one was commanded by Sytor, whom I trusted, and included Teeaytan-ov, who often bragged loudly about his friendship for me. The part of the palace it was to search included the room in which Janai was hiding.

I did not direct the search particularly to that apartment, and I became extremely nervous while they searched everywhere but where she was. At last they came to the storeroom. I followed Sytor into it.

"She is not here," I said.

"But there is another door, over there," he replied, and walked over to it.

"Probably just another storeroom," I said, trying to appear indifferent, though my heart was pounding with excitement.

"It's locked," he said—"locked on the other side. This looks suspicious."

I stepped to his side and called, "Janai!" There was no reply. My heart sank. "Janai! Janai!" I repeated.

"She is not there,' said Sytor, "but I suppose we'll have to break the door down to make sure."

"Yes, break it down."

He sent for tools, and when they were brought his hormads set to work upon the door As the panels commenced to splinter, Janai's voice came from the interior of the other room. "I will open," she said. We heard the bolt being withdrawn, and then the door swung open. My heart leaped as I saw her there safe and well. "What do you want of me?" she demanded.

"I am to take you to Ay-mad, the Jeddak," said Sytor.

"I am ready," said Janai. She did not even look at me. I wondered if she had decided at last that it might not be so bad to be a jeddara. She had had many days to think the matter over, during which I had not visited her. Perhaps she had changed her mind. I could understand that the temptation might be great, for what had Vor Daj to offer her? Certainly not security, which is what a woman wants above all things.

Down to the private audience chamber of Ay-mad, Jeddak of Morbus, my heart trailed Sytor and Janai with its tail between its legs.

CHAPTER XIV

WHEN THE MONSTER GROWS

LOVE POSSESSES A morbid imagination which conjures the most appalling pictures. It cannot await the development of eventualities, but must anticipate the worst. Quite often it is clairvoyant. That was what I feared now as Sytor, Janai, and I stood before Ay-mad. Sytor, with his handsome face and fine body; Ay-mad in the trappings of a jeddak; Janai, perfect and beautiful! These I compared with my hideous face and monstrous, malformed body; and my heart sank. How could Janai choose me in preference to any normal man? And if that man were a jeddak, what chance would I have? I insisted on confusing myself with the real Vor Daj, and you must admit that it might be confusing to have one brain and two bodies

Ay-mad's eyes devoured Janai, and my heart quailed; but if she chose me, and Ay-mad failed to live up to his bargain, I swore to myself that I should kill him. He dismissed Sytor; then he faced Janai.

"This hormad," he said, indicating me, "has been of service to me. To reward him, I told him that I would grant him a favor. He has asked for you. We have decided that we shall abide by your choice. If Ras Thavas is found, the hormad hopes to acquire a new body. If Ras Thavas is not found, he will remain always as he is. If you choose me, you will become jeddara of Morbus. Whom do you choose?"

I could not but feel that Ay-mad had stated the case quite fairly, but I guess he felt that every argument was on his side anyway; so why add embellishments? In weighing the matter, there didn't seem much doubt as to what Janai's answer must be. Ay-mad was offering her marriage and position. Vor Daj had nothing to offer, and there was no more reason to suspect that her heart could be inclined more to one than to the other—she scarcely knew either.

Ay-mad became impatient. "Well," he demanded, "what is your answer?"

"I shall go with Tor-dur-bar," she said.

Ay-mad bit his lip, but he took it rather decently. "Very well," he said, "but I think you are making a mistake. If you change your mind, let me know." Then he dismissed us.

On the way back to the laboratory building I was walking on air. Janai had made her choice, and I should have her with me now and under my protection. She seemed rather happy, too.

"Shall I see Vor Daj right away?" she asked.

"I'm afraid not," I replied.

"Why?" she demanded, and she seemed suddenly depressed.

"It may take a little time," I explained. "In the mean time you will be with me and perfectly safe."

"But I thought that I was going to see Vor Daj. You haven't tricked me into this, have you, hormad?"

"If you think that, you had better go back to Ay-mad," I snapped, prompted by probably the strangest complexity of emotions that any human being had ever been assailed with—I was jealous of myself!

Janai became contrite. "I'm sorry," she said, "but I am terribly upset. Please forgive me. I have been through enough to drive one mad."

I had already selected and arranged quarters for Janai in the laboratory building. They were next to mine and some little distance from the horror of the vat rooms. I had selected several of the more intelligent hormads as her servants and guards, and she seemed quite pleased with the arrangements. When I had seen her safely established, I told her that if she needed me or wished to see me about anything to send for me and I would come; then I left her and went to Ras Thavas's study.

I had accomplished all of my design that required my hideous disguise; but now I could not rid myself of it; and it stood in the way of my aiding Janai to escape from Morbus, for I could not go out into the world in my present monstrous form. Only in Morbus could I hope for any safety.

To occupy my mind I had been looking through Ras Thavas's papers and notes, most of which were utterly meaningless to me; and now I continued idly going through his desk, though my mind was not on anything that I saw. I was thinking of Janai. I was wondering what had become of John Carter and Ras Thavas and what fate had overtaken my poor body. The future could not have looked darker. Presently I came upon what was evidently the plans of a building, and as I examined them casually I saw that they were the plans of the laboratory building, for I easily recognized the two floors with which I was most familiar.

At the bottom of the sheets was a floor plan of the pits beneath the building. It was laid out in corridors and cells. There were three long corridors running the length of the pits and five transverse corridors, and they were numbered from 1 to 8. The cells along each corridor were also numbered, even numbers upon one side of each corridor and odd numbers upon the other. It was all very uninteresting, and I rolled the plans up to replace them in the desk. Just then Tun Gan was announced by the guard in the outer room. He was quite excited when he came in.

"What's the matter?" I asked, for I could see by his manner that there was something wrong.

"Come here," he said, "and I'll show you."

He led me out into the main corridor and then into a side room that overlooked a large courtyard that gave light and ventilation to several of the inside rooms of the laboratory, among them No. 4 vat room, the windows of which were directly across from the room in which we were. The sight that met my eyes as I looked out into the courtyard was absolutely appalling. The mass of living tissue had grown so rapidly in the forcing culture medium discovered by Ras Thavas that it had completely filled the room, exerting such pressure in all directions that finally a window had given way; and the horrid mass was billowing out into the courtyard.

"There!" said Tun Gan. "What are you going to do about that?"

"There is nothing I can do about it," I said. "There is nothing that anybody can do about it. I doubt that Ras Thavas could do anything. He has created a force that he probably couldn't control himself, once it got away from him."

"What will be the end of it?" asked Tun Gan.

"If it doesn't stop growing it will crowd every other living thing out of Morbus. It grows and grows and feeds upon itself. It might even envelop the whole world. What is there to stop it?"

Tun Gan shook his head. He didn't know. "Maybe Aymad could stop it," he suggested. "He is jeddak."

"Send for him," I said. "Tell him that something has happened here in the laboratory building that I wish him to see for himself." For once in my life I was anxious to shift responsibility to another's shoulders, for I was helpless in the face of such an emergency as had never before confronted any human being since the creation of the world.

72

Well, in due time Ay-mad came; and when he had looked out of the window and listened to my explanation of the phenomenon he just tossed the whole responsibility back into my lap.

"You wanted to have full charge of the laboratory," he said, "and I put you in charge. This is your problem, not mine." With that he turned away and went back to the palace. By this time the entire floor of the courtyard was covered with the wriggling, jibbering mass; and more was oozing down from the broken window above.

Well, I thought, it will take a long time to fill this courtyard. In the meantime I may think of something to do, and with that I returned to my quarters and sat looking despondently out of the window across the walls of Morbus at the dismal Toonolian Marsh that spread in all directions as far as the eye could see. It reminded me of the spreading mass in the courtyard beneath No. 4 vat room; so I closed my eyes to shut out the sight.

For some reason, the plans of the building, that I had found in Ras Thavas's desk, came to my mind; then I recalled the trip from Helium with The Warlord. That reminded me of my own body, for I could see it now, trapped in the harness of The Warlord's Guards. Where was it? I had last seen it on the ersite slab in the small laboratory of Ras Thavas. That slab was empty now, and at its foot hung a single sheet with the cryptic numbers 3–17 written on it. 3–17! What in the world could that signify?

Suddenly my mind was galvanized into action. Those numbers might have definite significance! I leaped to my feet and hurried to Ras Thavas's little study. Here I dragged out the plans of the building and spread them out, turning back the pages to the floor plan of the pits. I ran my finger quickly down corridor 3 to 17. Could that be the answer? I examined the plans more carefully. In one corner of cell 17 was a tiny circle. There were no circles in any of the other cells. What did that circle mean? Did it mean anything? Did the "3–17" written on the sheet at the foot of the table on which my body had lain have any connection with a corridor and cell number? There was but one way to answer these questions. I rose hurriedly from the desk and went out into the corridor. Passing hormads and officers, I made my way to the ramp that led to the lower floor and the pits. I carried the map of the pits indelibly imprinted upon my memory. I could have found 3–17 with my eyes shut.

The corridors and the cells were plainly numbered; so that I had no difficulty in finding cell 17 in corridor 3. I tried the door. It was locked! How stupid of me. I might have known that it would be locked if it hid the thing for which I sought. I knew where Ras Thavas kept the keys to the various locks in the laboratory building; so now I retraced my steps, but this time I saw several officers look at me in what I imagined was a suspicious manner. Spies, I thought; some of Ay-mad's spies. I should have to be careful. That would mean further delay.

Now I moved listlessly. I pretended to inspect one of the vat rooms. I sent one of the officers I had long suspicioned on an errand. I went to a window and looked out. Eventually I made my leisurely way to the study; and here I had no difficulty in finding the key I sought, as Ras Thavas was meticulously methodical in all he did; and each key had been numbered and marked.

Now I must return to the pits without arousing suspicion. Once again I sauntered out through the corridors and rooms, and finally made my way to the ramp. Unobserved, I descended. At last I stood again before the door to 3–17. I fitted the key, took a last look up and down the corridor to assure myself that I was alone, and then pushed the door open. Like the corridors, the cell was lighted by means of the everlasting radium bulbs commonly used on Barsoom.

Directly before me, on a table, lay my body. I entered the cell and closed the door behind me. Yes, there was my body; and there the vessel containing my blood. We were all together again, my body, my blood, and my brains; but we were still as far apart as the poles. Only Ras Thavas could bring us together as an entity, and Ras Thavas was gone.

CHAPTER XV

I FIND MY MASTER

I STOOD FOR A long time looking at my body. I had never been a vain man, but when I compared it with the horrid thing that my brain now animated it seemed the most beautiful thing I had ever beheld. I thought of Janai in her apartments above, and cursed myself for a fool for ever

74

giving up the body that she might have loved for one that no creature could love.

But such repining was of no avail, and I forced myself to think of other things. The little circle that appeared in the plans of cell 17 came to my mind, and I walked to the corner of the room where it had indicated that something might be found different from what was in the construction of the other cells in the pits. There was something there. It was scarcely visible, but it was there—a faint line marking a circle about two feet in diameter. I got down on my hands and knees and examined it. At one side of it was a small indentation. The thing looked as though it might be a cunningly fitted trap door and the indentation a place to pry it open. I inserted the point of my dagger and pried. The trap rose easily. Presently it was high enough to permit me to get my fingers beneath it, and in another moment I had lifted it to one side revealing a dark void beneath. What lay there? What was the purpose of the opening?

There was only one way to find out. I lowered my body through the aperture which was but barely large enough to accommodate my gross carcass. When I was hanging at the full length of my long right arm my toes just touched something solid. I hoped it was the bottom of the pit, and let go.

I stood now on a solid flooring. The little light that came through the aperture above me showed me a narrow corridor leading away into utter darkness. There was nothing for me to do but explore, now that I had come this far. I wished that I might have returned the cover to its place; so that if any one should come to the cell they might not discover the trap door; then I commenced to wonder just how any one could get out of this place if the cover were closed above them. Open, a man could jump for the edge of the opening and draw himself up; but closed, he simply couldn't get out.

There was something wrong here. There must be some other way. I commenced to grope about searching for it, whatever it was; and at last I found it—a pole resting on pegs near the top of the corridor. By resting it against the edge of the aperture, I climbed up and dragged the cover almost into position; then I descended and, with the pole, poked the cover into place.

Now I started groping my way through utter darkness along the corridor. I felt ahead with a toe before taking a single step, and I kept my hands on both sides of the corridor lest I miss some forking or crossing corridor that might throw me off my track when I returned—if ever I did return. That thought gave me pause. What would happen to Janai if I failed to return? Perhaps I shouldn't continue on this new adventure. Perhaps I should go back. But no After all, it was in her interests that I was thus exploring beneath the pits of Morbus. Perhaps here was an avenue to freedom.

On and on I went. The floor of the corridor was level and there were no forks nor cross corridors. It curved a little twice, but not much. I kept thinking, well, I must be nearly to the end of it; but on and on it went The walls became damp, and the corridor stunk of mold; and then I came to a sharp declivity. For a moment I hesitated, but only for a moment. The floor inclined downward at an angle of some 15°, and by the time I reached level going again I must have been thirty or forty feet below the original level. The walls and ceiling dripped moisture. The floor was slimy with it. I walked on and on along this black, interminable tunnel. I thought it would never end; and when it did, as it must, into what new predicament would I find that it had lured me? Sometimes I thought of turning back, but that was only because I thought of Janai and her dependence upon me.

"Hormad!" I could still hear her calling me that, and I could feel the contempt and loathing that she could not have entirely hidden had she tried. And the way she spoke of Vor Daj in the same breath, and the way her voice changed! Once again a wave of jealousy of myself swept over me; but my sense of humor came to my rescue, and I laughed. That laugh resounded in the corridor, sepulchral and eerie. I didn't laugh again—it was too horrible.

Now the floor of the corridor was rising again. Up and up until I felt that I must have gained the original level; and then, suddenly, I saw light ahead, or rather lesser darkness; and a moment later I stepped out into the open. It was night. Neither moon was in the sky. Where was I? I realized that I had travelled miles, perhaps, through that gloomy corridor. I must be outside the walls of Morbus, but where?

Suddenly a figure loomed before me, and in the dim light I saw that it was a hormad. "Who are you?" it demanded. "What are you doing here?" and without waiting for an answer it came for me with a longsword.

That was language I understood, and had an answer to. I drew and engaged the thing. It was a better swordsman than any I had previously engaged. It knew some tricks that

I thought only the pupils of John Carter knew. When it discovered that I had the solution of all its tricks, it let out a yell; and in a moment or two three other figures came barging out of the night. The leader was no hormad, but a tall red man. He had scarcely engaged me before I recognized him.

"John Carter!" I cried. "It is I, Vor Daj."

Instantly he dropped his point and stepped back. "Vor Daj!" he exclaimed. "In the name of my first ancestor, how did you get here?"

Ras Thavas and a second hormad came up, and I told them briefly how I had discovered the 17th cell and the opening into the corridor.

"And now tell me," I said, "what you are doing here."

"Let Ras Thavas tell you," said The Warlord.

"Morbus is an ancient city," said the great surgeon. "It was built in prehistoric times by a people who are now extinct. In my flight after our defeat at Toonol I discovered it. I have remodeled and rebuilt it, but largely upon the foundations of the old city, which was splendidly built. There is much about it of which I know nothing. There were plans of many of the buildings, including those of the laboratory building. I noticed that circle in cell 17, just as you did. I thought it meant something, but never had the time or inclination to investigate. When we decided to hide your body where it could not be found and destroyed if anything went wrong, I selected cell 17, with the result that we discovered the tunnel to this island which lies fully two miles from Morbus.

"Dur-dan and Il-dur-en carried your body down to cell 17, and we brought them with us. They are two of my best hormads, intelligent and loyal. Having escaped from Morbus, we decided to attempt to make our way to the west end of the Great Toonolian Marsh, recover John Carter's flier, and fly to Helium in the hope that I might arrive in time to save Dejah Thoris from death.

"We have been occupied in building a boat for the long journey through the marsh, and it is about completed. We were in a quandry as to what to do about you. We did not want to desert you; but as the flier will accommodate but two men, you would have to be left somewhere until we could return; and you were safer in Morbus than you would have been in the hills beyond Phundahl."

"You shouldn't have given me a thought," I said. "Our sole objective was to find you and get you back to Helium as quickly as possible. I knew when we set out that I should have to be left behind when you were located. as the flier is not designed for more than two. That would have been a small sacrifice to have made for the Princess of Helium. The Warlord would have sent for me later."

"Naturally," said The Warlord. "Nevertheless, I hated to leave you here; but there was no alternative. We planned to send Il-dur-en back into the city with a message explaining everything to you. Dur-dan is to accompany us. If we manage to escape from the marsh and reach the flier, he will attempt to return to Morbus."

"When do you expect to start?" I asked.

"The boat will be finished tomorrow, and we shall set out as soon as it is dark. We plan to travel by night, resting and hiding during the daylight hours, as Ras Thavas, who is familiar with the marsh, assures me that it would be impossible for any but a large force of warriors to traverse the marsh by day. Many of the islands are inhabited by savage aborigines or by even more savage pirates and outlaws. The Great Toonolian Marshes are the last dregs of the great oceans that once covered a considerable portion of Barsoom, and the creatures which inhabit them are the last dregs of humanity."

"Is there any way in which I can be of help to you?" I asked.

"No," he said. "You have already sacrificed enough."

"Then I shall go back to the city before my absence is noticed. I have responsibilities there almost equal to your own, sir."

"What do you mean?" he asked.

"Janai," I said.

"What of her? Have you found her?"

I then told them of all that had transpired of which they knew nothing, that Ay-mad was jeddak and sole ruler of Morbus, that I was an odwar and in charge of the laboratory building, and that Janai had been given into my protection.

"So you are in charge of the laboratory building," said Ras Thavas. "How does it there in my absence?"

"Horribly," I said. "The only compensation for your absence is the fact that the production of hormads will have to cease, but we are faced now with something that may prove infinitely worse than hormads." Then I told him of what was transpiring in No. 4 vat room.

He appeared deeply concerned. "That is deplorable," he said. "It is something that I have always feared and sedulously guarded against. By all means make every preparation that you can to be prepared to escape from Morbus if you are unable to stem the growth in No. 4 vat room. Eventually it will envelop the entire island if it is not checked. Theoretically, it might cover the entire surface of Barsoom, smothering all other forms of life. It is the original life principal that cannot die, but it must be controlled. Nature controlled it, but I have learned to my sorrow that man cannot. I interfered with the systematic functioning of Nature; and this, perhaps, is to be my punishment."

"But how can I stem the growth? How can I stop this horror from spreading?" I demanded.

He shook his head. "There is but one thing, another phenomenon of Nature, that can check it."

"And that?" I asked.

"Fire," he said, "but evidently it has gone too far for that."

"I am afraid so," I said.

"About all that you can do now is to save yourself and Janai from it and wait for us to return."

"I shall come back with a sufficient force of men and ships to reduce Morbus and rescue you," said The Warlord.

"Until then, sir," I said. "And may you bring me word that the Princess of Helium has been restored to health."

CHAPTER XVI

THE JEDDAK SPEAKS

I WAS TERRIBLY DEPRESSED as I made my way back through that dark tunnel. It seemed to me that there was little likelihood that John Carter and Ras Thavas would live to reach the western extremity of the marshes. The Warlord would be dead, Dejah Thoris, my beloved princess, would be doomed to death. It seemed to me that then there would be nothing more to live for. Janai was already hopelessly lost to me so long as I was doomed to inhabit this repulsive carcass.

Yes, there was something to live for—Janai. At least I could dedicate my life to her protection. Possibly some day I might be able to engineer her escape from Morbus. Now that I knew of the tunnel my hopes in that direction were a little brighter.

At last I came to cell 17. Once more I delayed to gaze

wistfully and admiringly upon my poor corpse. Would my brain ever again animate it? I shrank to give answer to that question, as, with leaden feet, I left the cell and ascended to the upper floors. As I approached the study I was met by Tun Gan.

"I am glad you are back," he said with evident relief.

"Why? What is the matter? Something else gone wrong?"

"I don't know," he replied, "because I don't know where you have been or what you have been doing. Do you know if you were followed, or if anyone has seen you?"

"No one saw me," I said, "but then it would have made no difference if they had. I have merely been inspecting the pits." I wasn't taking any chances with the loyalty of any one. "But why do you ask?"

"Ay-mad's spies have been very active," he said. "I know some of them and suspect others. I think he has sent some new ones to watch you. They say he is furious because the woman chose to come with you rather than remain with him and become Jeddara of Morbus."

"You mean that they have been searching for me?" I asked.

"Yes; everywhere. They have even gone to the apartments of the woman."

"She is all right? They didn't take her away?"

"Not that I know of."

"But you don't know for certain?"

"No."

My heart sank. Could this have happened, too? I hurried toward Janai's apartments, and Tun Gan followed me. The fellow seemed almost as concerned as I. Perhaps he was all right. I hope so, for I needed every loyal ally that I could muster if Ay-mad were planning to take Janai away from me.

When the guard at the door recognized me, he stepped aside and let us enter. At first I did not see Janai. She was sitting with her back toward me, looking out of the window. I called her by name and she rose and turned. She appeared pleased to see me, but when her eyes passed me and alighted on Tun Gan they dilated with terror and she shrank back.

"What is that man doing here?" she demanded.

"He is one of my officers," I said. "What has he done? Has he offered you any harm while I was away?"

"Don't you know who he is?" she demanded.

"Why, he is Tun Gan. He is a good officer."

"He is Gantun Gur, the assassin of Amhor," she said. "He murdered my father."

"I realized at once the natural mistake she had made. "It is only Gantun Gur's body," I said. "His brain has been burned. The brain he now has is the brain of a friend."

"Oh," she said, relieved. "Some more of the work of Ras Thavas. Forgive me, Tun Gan; I did not know."

"Tell me about the man whose body is now mine," said Tun Gan.

"He was a notorious assassin of Amhor often employed by the prince, Jal Had. Jal Had wanted me, but my father would not give me up. He knew that I would rather die than be the wife of Jal Had; so Jal Had employed Gantun Gur to assassinate my father and abduct me. I managed to escape, and was on my way to Ptarth where my father had friends. Gantun Gur followed me. He had with him a strong party of assassins, all members of the Assassins' Guild. They overtook us and attacked the little party of loyal retainers that had accompanied me into exile. Night came on while they were still fighting, and my party was scattered. I never saw any of them again, and two days later I was captured by hormads. I suppose Gantun Gur was captured later by another party."

"You need never fear him again," I said.

"It seems strange, though, to see him just as I knew him and yet to realize that it is not he."

"There are many strange things in Morbus," I said. "Not all of those you see have the brains or the bodies which originally belonged to them."

It was strange, indeed. Here stood Tun Gan with the body of Gantun Gur and the brain of Tor-dur-bar, and I with the body of Tor-dur-bar and the brain of Vor Daj. I wondered what Janai's reaction would be if she knew the truth. If she had loved Vor Daj, I should have explained everything to her, for it would have been better then for her to know the truth; but not loving him, and there was no reason to believe that she might, my present form might have so revolted her that she could never love me even should I regain my own body. That is the way I reasoned, and so I determined not to tell her.

I explained to her why Tun Gan and I had come to her apartments and that she must be very careful of her every word and act inasmuch as she was doubtless surrounded by the spies and informers of Ay-mad.

She looked at me questioningly for a moment; and then she

81

said, "You have been very good to me. You are the only friend I have. I wish that you would come to see me oftener. You do not have to make excuses or explanations for coming. Do you bring me any word of Vor Daj this time?"

My spirits had risen at the first part of her speech, but with the last sentence I felt that incomprehensible jealousy come over me. Could it be that the body of Tor-dur-bar was so merging with the brain of Vor Daj as to absorb the identity of the latter? Could I be falling in love with Janai as a hormad? And if so what might the outcome be? Might I not come so to hate and fear Vor Daj that I might destroy his body because Janai loved it better than she did the body of Tor-dur-bar? The idea was fantastic, but so were all of the conditions surrounding it.

"I bring you no word of Vor Daj," I said, "because he has disappeared. Perhaps if we knew what had become of Dotar Sojat and Ras Thavas, we might know what has become of Vor Daj."

"You mean that you do not know where Vor Daj is?" she demanded. "Tor-dur-bar, there is something strange about all this. I want to trust you, but you have been very evasive about Vor Daj since first you came to me. I feel that you are trying to keep me from seeing him. Why?"

"You are mistaken," I said. "You will have to trust me, Janai. When I can, I shall bring you and Vor Daj together again. That is all that I can say. But why are you so anxious to see Vor Daj?"

I thought I might surprise her into saying something that would give a hint as to her feelings toward Vor Daj. I didn't know whether I hoped or feared that she might give some indications of affection for him, so confused were all the re-actions of my dual personality. But my ruse was of no avail. Her reply suggested nothing.

"He promised to help me escape," she said. That was all. Her interest in Vor Daj was purely selfish. However, that was better than no interest at all. Thus, I thought, love reasons, making a fool of a man, until it occurred to me that my interest in Janai might be purely selfish, too. There was little to choose between the two. She wanted her liberty; I wanted her. The question was, would I risk everything, even my life, to gain her liberty for her, knowing that I should lose her? Well, I knew that I would, so perhaps my love was not entirely selfish. It pleased me to think that it was not.

I noticed, as we talked, that two of the hormad servants were watching us closely, edging nearer and nearer, obviously endeavoring to overhear what we were saying. That they were a couple of Ay-mad's spies, I had no doubt; but their technique was so crude as to render them almost harmless. I cautioned Janai against them in a low tone; and then, as they came within earshot, I said to her, "No, there is no use; I won't permit you to leave your quarters; so don't ask me again. You are much safer here. You see you belong to me now, and I have the right to kill any one who might threaten to harm you. I should do it, too." This was for the benefit of the spies.

I left her then and took Tun Gan with me. Back again in the study, I reached a decision. I must surround myself and Janai with loyal followers, but in order to attempt this I must take some chances. I sounded Tun Gan out. He said he owed everything to Vor Daj and Ras Thavas, and as they were both my friends he would serve me in any way that he could. He had no love for any of the jeds.

During the next two days I talked with Sytor, Pandar, Gan Had, and Teeaytan-ov, and became convinced that I could depend upon their loyalty. I succeeded in having all but Teeaytan-ov transferred to duty in the laboratory building where more officers were needed in an attempt to stem the spread of the horrific growth billowing from No. 4 vat room. Teeaytan-ov was to serve me as a spy in the palace. Sytor was the officer who had been in command of the hormads which had captured The Warlord and me. I had rather liked him, and after talking with him at some length I became convinced that he was a normal red man in possession of his own brain, for he was familiar with places and events of the outer world that no hormad could have had knowledge of. He was from Dusar, and anxious to escape Morbus and return to his own country.

Pandar was the man from Phundahl, and Gan Had the man from Toonol who had been my fellow prisoners; so I knew something about them. They both assured me that if I were truly serving Vor Daj and Dotar Sojat they would work with me willingly.

All of these men thought, of course, that I was only a hormad; but my rank assured them that I had influence and that I was an important person. I explained to them that I had been promised the body of a red man as soon as Ras Thavas was located and that then I should be one of them and anxious to leave Morbus.

The growth of the tissue in No. 4 vat room had now almost filled the large courtyard. I had had all windows and doors opening from the enclosure securely barricaded, so that it could not enter the building, but it threatened to soon top it and flow across the roofs where it would eventually find its way into the city avenues. The production of new hormads had practically ceased, and I had drained all the tanks as they were emptied so that there might be no repetition of what had occurred in No. 4 vat room. This had necessitated my visiting every building in which there were culture tanks, and there were many of them. It was on my return from one of these other buildings that I received a summons to appear before Ay-mad.

As I entered the palace Teeaytan-ov came to meet me. "Be careful," he warned. "Something is afoot. I don't know what it is, but one of Ay-mad's servants said that he was always muttering about you and the woman. Now that he has lost her she seems even more desirable than before. If you want to save yourself trouble, you had better give her back to him; for if you don't he can have you killed and take her anyway, and no woman is worth that."

I thanked him and went on into the audience chamber where all of Ay-mad's principal officers were gathered before the throne. The jeddak greeted me with a scowling countenance as I took my place among the other officers, the only one without the body of a red man. How many hormad brains there were among them, I had no way of knowing; but from what I had heard since coming to Morbus I guessed that most of them were transplanted hormad brains. They would have been surprised, and Ay-mad most of all, could they have known that behind my hideous hormad face lay the brain of a noble of Helium and a trusted aide of The Warlord of Barsoom.

Ay-mad pointed a finger at me. "I trusted you," he said. "I put you in charge of the laboratories, and what have you done? The supply of warriors has ceased."

"I am not Ras Thavas," I reminded him.

"You have permitted the catastrophe of No. 4 vat room, which threatens to overwhelm us."

"Again let me remind you that I am not The Master Mind of Mars," I interrupted.

He paid no attention to that, but went on. "These things threaten the collapse of all our plans to conquer the world and necessitate an immediate attempt to launch our campaign with inadequate forces. You have failed in the laboratory; and I now relieve you of your duties there, but I shall give you another chance to redeem yourself. It is now my intention to conquer Phundahl at once, thus acquiring a fleet of ships with which we can transport warriors to Toonol. The capture of Toonol will give us additional ships and permit us to move on to the capture of other cities. I am placing you in command of the expedition against Phundahl. It will not require a large force to take that city. We have five hundred malagors. They can make two round trips a day. That means that you can transport a thousand warriors a day to a point near Phundahl; or, if the birds can carry double, two thousand. In the same way you can place a thousand warriors inside the city walls to take and open the gates to the main body of your troops. You will first transport the vats and culture medium necessary to produce food for your warriors. With twenty thousand warriors you can make your attack; and I will continue to send you two thousand a day until the campaign is over, for you will lose many. You will immediately give up your quarters in the laboratory building and take quarters here in the palace that I shall assign to you and your retinue."

I saw immediately what he was trying to accomplish. He would get Janai transferred to the palace and then he would send me out on the campaign against Phundahl.

"You will move to the palace immediately and commence the transport of your troops forthwith. I have spoken."

CHAPTER XVII

ESCAPE US NEVER

I NOW FOUND MYSELF faced by a problem for which there seemed no solution. Had I been in possession of my own body I could have escaped with Janai through the tunnel to the island where John Carter and Ras Thavas had hidden and waited there for their return, but I couldn't abandon my body and chance having to go out into the world a hormad. I also felt that it was my duty as a red man to remain and attempt in some way to thwart Ay-mad's plan of world conquest. As I made my way to Janai's quarters to tell her what had befallen us my spirits had reached nadir; they could fall no lower.

As I was passing along a corridor in the laboratory building I was met by Tun Gan who seemed very much perturbed. "The mass from No. 4 vat room has crossed the roof in one place and is overflowing down the side of the building into the avenue," he said. "The growth seems suddenly to have accelerated; and, if it be not stopped, it is only a question of time before it envelops the entire city."

"And the island as well," I said, "but I can do nothing about it; Ay-mad has relieved me of my duties in the laboratory. The responsibility now belongs to my successor."

"But what can we do to save ourselves?" demanded Tun Gan. "We shall all be lost if the growth be not stopped. It has already seized and devoured several of the warriors who were sent to try to destroy it. The hands reach out and seize them, and the heads devour them. Eventually it will eat us all."

Yes, what could we do to save ourselves? For the moment ourselves included only Janai and my two selves in my thoughts, but presently I thought of others—of Pandar and Gan Had and Sytor, yes, even of Tun Gan, the assassin of Amhor, with the brain of a hormad. These men were as near to being friends as any I had in Morbus, and there was poor Teeaytan-ov, too. He had been my friend. I must save them all.

"Tun Gan," I said, "you would like to escape?"

"Of course."

"Will you swear to serve me loyally if I help you to get away from Morbus, forgetting that you are a hormad?"

"I am no hormad now," he said. "I am a red man, and I will serve you loyally if you will help me to escape from the clutches of the horror that is spewing out into the city."

"Very well. Go at once to Pandar and Gan Had and Sytor and Teeaytan-ov and tell them to come to the quarters of Janai. Caution them to secrecy. Let no one overhear what you say to them. And hurry, Tun Gan!"

I went at once to the quarters of Janai, who seemed glad to see me; and told her of Ay-mad's orders that we move to quarters in the palace. The two servants whom I suspected overheard, as I intended they should; and I immediately gave them orders to gather up their mistress's belongings, which gave me an opportunity to talk with Janai privately. I told her what Ay-mad's order portended and that I had a plan which offered some slight hope of escape.

"I will take any risk," she said, "rather than remain in Ay-mad's palace after you are sent away. You are the only person in Morbus that I can trust, my only friend; though why you befriend me, I do not know."

"Because Vor Daj is my friend and Vor Daj loves you," I

said. I felt like a coward, adopting this way of avowing a love I might not have had the courage to tell her had I been in possession of my own identity; and now that I had done it I immediately wished that I hadn't. What if she scorned Vor Daj's love? He would not be here in person to press his suit, and certainly a hideous hormad could not do it for him. I held my breath as I waited for her reply.

She was silent for a moment, and then she asked. "What makes you think that Vor Daj loves me?"

"I think it was perfectly obvious. He could not have been so concerned over the fate of any woman if he had not loved her."

"You are probably mistaken. Vor Daj would have been concerned over the fate of any red woman who might have been a prisoner in Morbus. How could there be love between us? We scarcely know one another; we have spoken only a few words together."

I was about to argue the point when Pandar, Gan Had, and Sytor arrived, putting an end to the conversation and leaving me in as much doubt as to the feelings of Janai toward Vor Daj as I had been before. As these three had been employed in the laboratory building, Tun Gan had found them quickly. I sent them to my study to wait for me, as I did not wish to talk to them where we might be overheard by one of Ay-mad's spies.

A few minutes later Tun Gan returned with Teeaytan-ov, and the roster of those whom I hoped would aid me loyally was completed. By this time the servants had gathered Janai's belongings, which I ordered them to take to the palace to our new quarters; and in this way I got rid of them.

As soon as they had gone, I hurried to my study with Janai, Tun Gan, and Teeaytan-ov, where we found the other members of my party awaiting us. We were all together now, and I explained that I planned to escape from Morbus and asked each one if he were willing to accompany me. Each assured me that he did; but Sytor voiced a doubt, which I suppose each of them harbored, that escape would be possible.

"What is your plan?" he asked.

"I have discovered an underground corridor that leads to an island off the shore of Morbus," I said. "It was to this island that Dotar Sojat and Ras Thavas went when they disappeared from the city. They are on their way to Helium now, and you may rest assured that Dotar Sojat will return with a fleet of warships and a sufficient force of warriors to rescue me from Morbus."

Teeaytan-ov appeared skeptical. "Why," he asked, "should Dotar Sojat wish to rescue a hormad from Morbus?"

"And how," inquired Sytor, "can Dotar Sojat, a poor panthan, hope to persuade the jeddak of Helium to send a fleet of warships to the Toonolian Marshes for a hormad?"

"I admit," I replied, "that the idea appears fantastic; but that is because you do not know all the facts, and there are reasons why I do not wish to divulge them all at this time. Upon one point, however, I may set your minds at rest. That is the ability of Dotar Sojat to bring a fleet of warships from Helium. Dotar Sojat is, in reality, John Carter, Warlord of Mars."

This statement rather astounded them; but after I had explained why John Carter had come to Morbus, they believed me. Teeaytan-ov was still at a loss, however, to understand why the great Warlord should be so interested in a hormad as to bring a great fleet all the way from far Helium to rescue him.

I saw that I had made a mistake in speaking as I had, but it was sometimes difficult for me to disassociate my dual personalities. To me, I was always Vor Daj, a noble of the empire of Helium. To others, I was Tor-dur-bar, a hormad of Morbus.

"Perhaps," I said, seeking to explain, "I overemphasized my own importance when I said that he would return to rescue me. It is for Vor Daj that he will return; but for me, too, as both he and Vor Daj are my friends."

"What makes you think that he will rescue any of the rest of us?" asked Pandar of Phundahl.

"He will rescue anyone that Vor Daj asks him too; and that means anyone I suggest, for Vor Daj is my friend."

"But Vor Daj has disappeared," said Gan Had of Toonol. "No one knows what has become of him. It is thought that he is dead."

"You had not told me that, Tor-dur-bar," exclaimed Janai. She turned to Sytor. "Perhaps this is a trick the hormad is playing on us to get us in his power for some reason."

"But I did tell you that he had disappeared, Janai," I said.

"You did not tell me that everyone thought him dead. You say you do not know where he is in the same breath that you say John Carter will return for him. What am I to believe?"

"If you hope to live and escape you will have to believe

88

me," I snapped. "In a few minutes you will see Vor Daj, and then you will understand why he could not come to you." I was commencing to lose my patience with them all, interposing suspicions at a moment when the greatest haste was necessary if we were to escape before the suspicions of Aymad were aroused.

"What am I to believe?" demanded Janai. "You do not know where Vor Daj is, yet you say that we shall see him in a few minutes."

"There was a time that I did not know where he was. When I found him it seemed kinder to you, who were depending on him, not to tell you the truth. Vor Daj is helpless to aid you. Only I can help you. Unfortunately, in order to carry out my plan of escape, you will have to learn what has happened to Vor Daj. Now, we have wasted enough time uselessly. I am going, and you are coming with me. I owe it to Vor Daj to help you. The others may do as they see fit."

"I will go with you," said Pandar. "We could not be worse off elsewhere than here."

They all decided to accompany me, Sytor reluctantly. He went and stood near Janai and whispered something to her.

Taking Teeaytan-ov with me, I went into the small laboratory and collected all the instruments necessary to the retransfer of my brain to its own body. These I handed over to Teeaytan-ov; then I disconnected the motor and all its connections, for without the motor my blood could not be pumped back into my veins and arteries. All of this took time, but at last we were ready to depart.

I was quite sure that we could avoid neither notice nor suspicion. The best I could hope for was that we might reach 3-17 before pursuit overtook us. The spectacle of two hormads, four red men, and Janai, together with the burdens Teeaytan-ov and I were carrying, attracted immediate attention; and from no less a figure, among others, than the new governor of the Laboratory Building.

"Where are you going?" he demanded. "What are you going to do with that equipment?"

"I'm going to put it in the pits where it will be safe," I said. "If Ras Thavas returns he will need it."

"It will be safe enough where it was," he replied. "I'm in charge here now, and if I want it moved I'll attend to it myself. Take it back to where you got it."

"Since when did a dwar give orders to an odwar?" I asked. "Stand aside!" Then I moved on again, with my companions toward the ramp leading to the pits.

"Wait!" he snapped. "You're going nowhere with that equipment and the girl without an order from Ay-mad. You have your orders to take the girl to the palace, not to the pits; and I have my orders direct from Ay-mad to see that you obey yours." Then he raised his voice and shouted for help. I knew that we would soon be beset by warriors; so I directed my companions to hurry on toward the pits.

We fairly ran down the long winding incline with the Governor of the Laboratory Building at our heels keeping up a continuous bellowing for help; and behind us, presently, we heard the answering shouts of pursuing warriors.

CHAPTER XVIII

TREASON ISLAND

MY WHOLE PLAN now seemed to be doomed to failure, for even though we succeeded in reaching 3–17 I would not dare enter it and reveal the avenue for our escape. We had come this far, however; and there could be no turning back. There was only one solution to our problem: no witness must remain to carry back a report to Ay-mad.

We had reached the pits and were moving along the main corridor The Governor was dogging our footsteps but keeping a safe distance from us. The shouts of the pursuing warriors evidenced the fact that they were still on our trail. I called to Tun Gan to come to my side where I imparted my instructions to him in a low tone, after which he left me and spoke briefly to Teeaytan-ov and Pandar; then these three turned off into a side corridor. The Governor hesitated a moment, but did not follow them. His interest lay in keeping track of Janai and me, and so he followed on behind us. At the next intersecting corridor I led the remainder of the party to the right, halting immediately and laying aside my burden.

"We will meet them here," I said. "There is just one thing to remember: if we are to escape and live not one of those who are pursuing us must be left alive to lead others after us."

Sytor and Gan Had took their stand beside me. Janai remained a few paces behind us. The Governor stopped well out of sword's reach to await his warriors. There were no firearms among us, as the materials necessary to the fabrications of explosives either did not exist in the Toonolian Marshes or had not as yet been discovered there. We were armed only with longswords, shortswords, and daggers.

We did not have long to wait before the warriors were upon us. There were nine of them, all hormads. The Governor had the body of a red man and the brain of a hormad. I had known him fairly well in the palace. He was cunning and cruel, but lacked physical courage. He halted his warriors and the ten of them stood facing us.

"You had better surrender," he said, "and come back with me. You have no chance. There are ten of us and only three of you. If you will come quietly, I will say nothing to Aymad about this."

I saw that he was anxious to avoid a fight, but in a fight lay our only chance of escape. Once in the palace of Aymad, Janai and I would be lost. I pretended to be considering his proposition as I wished to gain a moment's time; and needed but a moment, as presently I saw Tun Gan, Pandar, and Teeaytan-ov closing silently up behind the Governor and his party.

"Now!" I cried, and at my word the three behind them let out a yell that caused the ten to turn simultaneously; then Sytor, Gan Had, and I leaped in with drawn swords. Numerically, the odds were all in their favor; but really they had no chance. The surprise attack disconcerted them, but the factors that gave the greatest advantage were my superhuman strength and my long sword arm. However, they soon realized that they were fighting for their lives; and, like cornered rats, they fought furiously.

I saw poor Teeaytan-ov go down with a cleft skull and Pandar wounded, but not until he had disposed of one antagonist; Tun Gan accounted for two. Sytor, to my surprise and disappointment, held back, not offering to risk himself; but we did not need him. One after another my longsword cleft skulls from crown to chin, until the only foe remaining was the Governor who had taken as little part in the brief affair as possible. Now, screaming, he sought to escape; but Tun Gan barred his way. There was a momentary clash of steel, a shriek; and then Tun Gan jerked his blade from the heart of the Governor of the Laboratory Building and wiped it in the hair of his fallen foe.

The corridor was a shambles in which horrible, blood drenched, brainless bodies lunged about. What followed I hate to recall; but it was necessary to destroy them all completely, especially their brains, before we could feel safe in continuing on our way.

Instructing Tun Gan to carry the articles that I had entrusted to Teeaytan-ov, I picked up the motor and led the way to 3–17. I noticed that Sytor walked close to Janai, conversing with her in low tones; but at the moment my mind was too preoccupied with other matters to permit this to assume any particular importance. So far we had been successful. What the future held for us, who could foresee? What means of subsistence there might be on the island, I did not know; nor had I more than the vaguest of plans as to how we might escape from the vicinity of Morbus and from the Great Toonolian Marshes in the event that John Carter failed to return for me. Only his death, I was sure, would prevent that; and I could not conceive that the great Warlord might die. To me, as to many others, he seemed immortal. But suppose he did return and without Ras Thavas? That thought filled me with horror, leaving me no alternative than self-destruction should it prove a true prophesy. Far better death than life in my present hideous and repulsive form. Better death than that Janai should be lost to me forever. Such were my thoughts as we reached the door to 3–17 and, swinging it open, I ushered my party into the chamber.

When Janai saw the body of Vor Daj lying on the cold ersite slab, she voiced an exclamation of horror and turned fiercely upon me. "You have lied to me, Tor-dur-bar," she said, in a suppressed whisper. "All the time you knew that Vor Daj was dead. Why have you done this cruel thing to me?"

"Vor Daj is not dead," I said. "He only awaits the return of Ras Thavas to restore him to life."

"But why didn't you tell me?" she asked.

"Only I knew where the body of Vor Daj was hidden. It would have profited neither you nor him had you known; and the fewer who knew, the safer was the body of Vor Daj. Not even to you, whom I knew that I could trust, would I divulge the secret of his hiding-place. Only now do you and these others know because there was no other avenue of escape from Morbus except through this room where Vor Daj lies. I believe that I can trust you all with this secret, but even so I can promise you that none of you will ever return alive to Morbus while the body of Vor Daj lies here and I remain alive."

Sytor had moved close to the slab where the body lay, and had been examining it rather minutely. I saw him nod his head and a half smile touched his lips as he shot a quick glance in my direction. I wondered if he suspected the truth; but what difference did it make if he did so long as he kept his mouth shut. I did not want Janai to know that the brain of Vor Daj abode in the hideous skull of Tor-dur-bar. Foolishly, perhaps, I thought that were she to know, she might never be able to forget the fact even when my brain was returned to its own body. She seemed emersed in thought for a few moments after I explained to her why I had not told her of the seeming tragedy that had overwhelmed Vor Daj; but presently she turned to me again and spoke kindly. "I am sorry that I doubted you, Tor-dur-bar," she said. "You did well in revealing to no one the whereabouts of Vor Daj's body. It was a wise precaution, and an act of loyalty."

CHAPTER XIX

NIGHT FLIGHT

IT WAS WITH a feeling of relief that I led my little party through the long tunnel to the rocky island off the shore of Morbus. How we were to escape from the island was a problem for the future. There was, of course, uppermost in my mind always the hope that John Carter would return from Helium with a rescuing fleet; but behind this hope lurked the spectre of fear engendered by the doubt as to whether he and Ras Thavas had been able to traverse the hideous wastes of the great Toonolian Marshes and reach his swift flyer that lay hidden beyond Phundahl.

There were birds and rodents on the island, and there grew there trees and shrubs which bore nuts and berries. All these, together with the fish that we were able to catch, furnished us with sufficient food so that we did not suffer from hunger but had an abundance. I had a shelter constructed for Janai so that she might enjoy some privacy; but as the weather was mild, the rest of us slept out.

The little island was hilly, and we made our camp upon the far side away from Morbus so that the hills would hide us from discovery from the city. In this secluded spot, I started construction of two light boats, each capable of carrying three of us and a supply of provisions, one being larger than the other for the purpose of accommodating Vor Daj's body, as I had determined to take it with us in the event that John Carter did not return within a reasonable time and it became necessary for us to attempt the perilous voyage in our frail craft.

During this period, I noticed that Sytor spent much of his leisure time in the company of Janai. He was a personable fellow and a clever conversationalist; so I could not wonder that she found pleasure in his company; yet I must admit that I suffered many pangs of jealousy. Sytor was also very friendly with Pandar, the Phundahlian; so that socially we seemed naturally to split into parties, with Pandar, Sytor and Janai in one, and Gan Had, Tun Gan and I in the other. There was no unpleasantness between any of us; but the division was more or less a natural one. Gan Had was a Toonolian; and Toonol and Phundahl were hereditary enemies, so that Gan Had and Pandar had little or nothing in common. Tun Gan, with the body of a red man and the brain of a hormad, and I, with the body of a hormad, possibly felt drawn to one another because we knew that the others in the secret recesses of their hearts considered us monsters, less human than the lower animals. I can tell you that a hideous body such as mine induces a feeling of inferiority that cannot be overcome; and Tun Gan, while he made a bold front with the body of the assassin of Amhor, must have felt much as I did.

After we had completed the boats, which required several weeks of unremitting labor, enforced idleness weighed heavily upon us, and dissension showed its ugly visage upon us. Sytor insisted that we start out at once, but I wished to wait a little longer as I knew that if John Carter lived and reached Helium, he would return for me. Pandar agreed with Sytor; but Gan Had demurred, as the plan was to try to reach Phundahl where he feared that he would be held prisoner and thrown into slavery. In the many arguments which ensued I had Tun Gan's backing and, to my great satisfaction, that of Janai also when she found that I was determined to wait yet a little longer.

"We should not leave," she said, "unless we can take Vor Daj's body with us, and this Tor-dur-bar refuses to permit until he himself is satisfied that there is no hope of rescue from Helium. I think, however," she said to me, "that you are making a mistake, and that you should bow to the superior judgment and experience of Sytor, who is a red man with a brain of a red man."

Sytor was present during this conversation, and I saw him shoot a quick glance at me; and again I wondered if he suspected that the brain of Vor Daj abode in my hideous head. I hoped he would not impart his suspicions to Janai.

"Sytor may have the brain of a red man," I said, "but it is functioning now only in the interest of Sytor. Mine, however inferior, is imbuded with but a single desire, which outweighs every other consideration than the welfare of you and Vor Daj. I shall not leave this island until the return of John Carter, unless I am absolutely forced to do so, until I am convinced that there remains no slightest hope that he will return; nor shall I permit you, Janai, to leave; the others may leave if they please, but I promised Vor Daj that I would protect Janai, and I should not be protecting her if I permitted her to undertake the perilous voyage through the Great Toonolian Marshes toward inhospitable Phundahl until there remains no alternative course to pursue."

"I am my own mistress," retorted Janai, angrily, "and I shall leave if I wish; no hormad may dictate to me."

"Janai is quite right," said Sytor. "You have no right to interfere."

"Nevertheless, I shall interfere," I replied, "and she shall remain here with me even if I have to keep her by force, which, I think you will all admit, I am physically able to do."

Well, things were not very pleasant after that; and Janai, Sytor and Pandar spent more time than ever together, and were often conversing in low tones that could not be overheard. I thought that they were only grumbling among themselves and heaping abuse upon me. Of course, it made me very blue to think that Janai had turned against me; and I was extremely unhappy; but I anticipated no other outcome from their grumblings than this and was quite confident that I should have my own way, which my better judgment convinced me was the safe way.

Sytor and Pandar had found a place to sleep that was quite a distance removed from the spot that Gan Had, Tun Gan, and I had selected, as though they would impress upon us that they had nothing in common with us. This suited me perfectly, as I had come to suspect and dislike both of them.

As I was preparing to retire one night after a day of fishing, Tun Gan came and squatted down beside me. "I overheard something today," he said, "which may interest you. I was dozing beneath a bush down by the beach this afternoon, when Sytor and Janai came and sat down beside the very bush behind which I had been dozing. They had evidently been discussing you, and I heard Janai say 'I am sure that he is really very loyal to Vor Daj and to me. It is only his judgment that is at fault; but what can one expect from the deformed brain of a hormad in such a deformed body?' "

" 'You are absolutely mistaken,' replied Sytor. 'He has only one idea in mind and that is to possess you for himself. There is something that I have known for a long time, but which I hesitated to tell you because I did not wish to hurt you. The Vor Daj that you knew will never live again. His brain was removed and destroyed, and Tor-dur-bar has hidden and protected his body, awaiting the return of Ras Thavas who will transfer Tor-dur-bar's hormad brain into the skull of Vor Daj. Then he will come to you with this new and beautiful body, hoping to win you; but it will not be Vor Daj who hopes to possess you, but the brain of a hormad in the body of a man.'

" 'How horrible!' exclaimed Janai. 'It cannot be true. How can you know such a thing?'

" 'Ay-mad told me,' replied Sytor. 'The body of Vor Daj was to be Tor-dur-bar's reward for the services that he had rendered Ay-mad; and to make assurance doubly sure Tor-dur-bar persuaded Ay-mad to have Vor Daj's brain destroyed.' "

"And what did Janai reply?" I asked. "She did not believe him, did she?"

"Yes, she believed him," said Tun Gan, "for she said that it explained many things that hitherto she had been unable to understand, and she now knew why you, a hormad, had evinced such remarkable loyalty toward a red man."

I was disgusted and angry and hurt, and I wondered if such a girl as Janai deserved the love and devotion that I had felt for her, and then my better judgment came to my rescue as I realized that Sytor's statement was, on the face of it, a logical explanation of my attitude toward the girl, for why indeed should a hideous hormad defend a red man whose body he might acquire, while at the same time acquiring a beautiful girl, or at least a reasonable chance of winning her such as his present hideous form would preclude.

"You see that you'll have to watch out for that rat," said Tun Gan.

"I shall not have to for long," I said, "for tomorrow I shall make him eat his words; and I shall tell them the truth, which I think Sytor already suspects, but will surprise Janai."

I lay awake for a long time that night wondering how Janai would react to the truth, what she would say or think or do when I told her that behind this hideous face of mine lay the brain of Vor Daj; but at last I fell asleep, and because I had lain awake so long I slept late the next morning. It was Gan Had of Toonol, who awoke me. He shook me roughly, and when I opened my eyes I saw that he was greatly excited.

"What's the matter, Gan Had?" I demanded.

"Sytor!" he explained. "Sytor and Pandar have taken one of the boats and escaped with Janai."

I leaped to my feet and ran quickly to where we had hidden the boats. One of them was gone; but that was not entirely the worst of it, for a big hole had been hacked in the bottom of the other which was bound to delay pursuit for several days.

So this was my reward for my love, loyalty, and devotion. I was very sick at heart. Now I did not care much whether John Carter returned or not. Life hereafter would be a void empty of all but misery. I turned disconsolately away from the boat. Gan Had laid a hand upon my shoulder.

"Do not grieve," he said. "If she went of her own volition, she is not worth grieving for."

At his words, a hope, a slender hope, just enough to grasp at in desperation came to relieve my mental agony. *If she went of her own volition!* Perhaps she did not go of her own volition. Perhaps Sytor took her away by force. There, at least, was a hope; and I determined to cling to it to the bitter end. I called to Tun Gan, and the three of us set to work to repair the damaged boat. We worked furiously, but it took three full days to make the craft seaworthy again, for Sytor had done an excellent job of demolition.

I guessed that because Pandar was with them, they would go direct to Phundahl where Pandar might succeed in having them received as friends; and so I planned to follow them to Phundahl, no matter what the cost. I felt within me the strength of a hundred men, the power to demolish a whole army single-handed, and to raze the walls of the strongest city.

At last we were ready to depart; but before we left I had one precaution to take. Beneath rocks and brush and dirt, I hid the entrance to the tunnel leading back to the room where Vor Daj's body lay.

Sytor had appropriated the larger boat, which was far more commodious for three people than would have been the smaller, but it was also heavier and there were only two men to paddle it, while in our lighter craft there were three of us. Gan Had, Tun Gan and myself; so notwithstanding the fact

97

that they had three days start of us, I felt that it was within the realm of possibility that we might overtake them before they reached Phundahl. This, however, was only a hope since it would be by the merest chance that we should follow the same course taken by them through the maze of winding waterways that lay between us and our destination. It was entirely possible that we might pass them without being aware of it. Either party might follow some fair-appearing stretch of water only to discover that it came to a blind end, necessitating the retracing of weary miles, for the wastes of the Toonolian Marshes are uncharted and were wholly unfamiliar to every member of both parties. Being accustomed to observing terrain from the air, I had obtained a fair mental picture of the area over which we had flown when the hormads had flown us to Morbus upon the backs of their malagors, and I had no doubt but that Sytor had flown over the district many times. However, I had little reason to believe that these facts would advantage either of us to any great extent, as from the surface of the water one's view was constantly obstructed by the vegetation which grew upon the surface of the marsh and by numerous islands, large and small.

My heart was indeed heavy as I set out in pursuit of Sytor; first, by my doubts as to the loyalty of Janai, and, second, because I was forced to abandon my own body and go into the world in the hideous disguise of a hormad. Why should I pursue Janai, who, listening to Sytor and believing him above me, had deserted me, may only be explained by the fact that I was in love with her, and that love makes a fool of a man.

We set forth after dark that we might escape detection from Morbus. Only Cluros, the smaller and farther moon, was in the sky, but it lighted our way sufficiently; and the stars gave us our direction, my prodigious strength adding at least two more man-power to the paddles. We had determined to push on both by day and by night, each obtaining what sleep he required, by turn, in the bottom of the boat. We had plenty of provisions, and the speed at which we could propel the canoe imbued us with the hope that we could escape the attack of any unfriendly natives who might discover us.

The first day a flock of malagors flew over us, traveling in the direction of Phundahl. We were concealed from them by the overhanging brush of a narrow canal we were traversing;

but they were plainly visible to us and we could see that each malagor carried a hormad warrior astride his back.

"Another raiding party," commented Gan Had.

"More likely a searching party that Ay-mad has dispatched in pursuit of us," I said, "for he must have discovered that we have escaped from Morbus."

"But we escaped weeks ago," said Tun Gan.

"Yes," I agreed, "but I have no doubt but that during all this time he has been sending searching parties in all directions."

Gan Had nodded. "Probably you are right. Let us hope that they do not discover any of us, for if they do we shall go to the vats or the incinerator."

On the second day after we had entered a fair-sized lake, we were discovered by savages who dwelt upon its shores. They manned a number of canoes and sallied forth to intercept us. We bent to our paddles, and our little craft fairly skimmed the surface of the water; but the savages had taken off from a point on the shore slightly ahead of us, and it seemed almost a certainty that they would reach us before we could pass them. They were a savage lot; and as they came closer, I saw that they were stark naked, their bushy hair standing out in all directions, their faces and bodies painted to render them more hideous even than Nature had intended them to be. They were armed with crude spears and clubs; but there was nothing crude about the manner in which they handled their long canoes, which sped over the water at amazing speed.

"Faster!" I urged. And now with every stroke our canoe seemed to leave the water, as it sprang ahead like a living thing.

The savages were yelling now in exultation, as it seemed certain that they must overhaul us; but the energy that they put into their savage cries had been better expended on their paddles, for presently we passed their leading boat and commenced to draw away from them. Furious, they hurled spears and clubs at us from the leading boat; but they fell short, and it was soon obvious that we had escaped them and they could not overtake us. They kept on however for a few minutes, and then, with angry imprecations, they turned sullenly back toward shore. It was well for us that they did so, for Gan Had and Tun Gan had reached the limit of their endurance, and both sank exhausted into the bottom of the canoe the moment that the savages gave up the pursuit. I felt no fatigue, and continued to paddle onward toward the end of the lake. Here we entered a winding canal which we followed for about two hours without further adventure. The sun was about to set when we heard the flapping of great wings approaching from ahead of us.

"Malagors," said Tun Gan.

"The searching party returns," remarked Gan Had; "with what success, I wonder."

"They are flying very low," I said. "Come, pull ashore under those bushes. Even so, we shall be lucky if they do not see us."

The bushes grew at the edge of a low, flat island that rose only a few inches above the surface of the water. The malagors passed over us low, and circled back.

"They are going to alight," said Tun Gan. "The hormads do not like to fly at night, for the malagors do not see well after dark, and Thuria, hurtling low above them, frightens and confuses them."

We were all looking up at them as they passed over us, and I saw that three of the malagors were carrying double.

The others noticed it too, and Gan Had said that they had prisoners.

"And I think that one of them is a woman," said Tun Gan.

"Perhaps they have captured Sytor and Pandar, and Janai."

"They are alighting on this island," said Gan Had. "If we wait until it is dark, we can pass them safely."

"First I must know if one of the prisoners is Janai," I replied.

"It will mean death for all of us if we are discovered," said Tun Gan. "We have a chance to escape, and we cannot help Janai by being captured ourselves."

"I must know," I said. "I am going ashore to find out; if I do not return by shortly after dark, you two go on your way, and may good luck attend you."

"And if you find that she is there?" asked Gan Had.

"Then I shall come back to you and we shall set out immediately for Morbus. If Janai is taken back, I must return too."

"But you can accomplish nothing," insisted Gan Had. "You will be sacrificing our lives as well as yours, uselessly. You have no right to do that to us when there is no hope of success. If there were even the slightest hope, it would be different; and I, for one, would accompany you; but as there is no hope, I flatly refuse. I am not going to throw my life away on a fool's errand."

"If Janai is there," I said, "I shall go back, if I have to

100

go back alone. You two may accompany me, or you may remain on this island. That is for you to decide."

They looked very glum, and neither made any reply as I crawled ashore among the concealing bushes. I gave no more thought to Tun Gan and Gan Had, my mind being wholly occupied with the problem of discovering if Janai were one of the prisoners the hormads were bringing back to Morbus. The low shrubs growing upon the island afforded excellent cover, and I wormed my way among them on my belly in the direction from which I heard voices. It was slow work, and it was almost dark before I reached a point from which I could observe the party. There were a dozen hormad warriors and two officers. Presently, creeping closer, I discovered some figures lying down, and immediately recognized the one nearest me as Sytor. He was bound, hand and foot; and by his presence I knew that Janai was there also; but I wished to make sure, and so I moved cautiously to another position from which I could see the other two. One of them was Janai.

I cannot describe the emotions that swept over me, as I saw the woman I loved lying bound upon the ground, again a prisoner of the hideous minions of Ay-mad, and doomed to be returned to him. She was so near to me, yet I could not let her know that I was there seeking a way to serve her as loyally as though she had not deserted me. I lay there a long time just looking at her, and then as darkness fell I turned and crawled cautiously away; but soon, as neither moon was in the heavens at the time, I arose without fear of detection and walked rapidly toward the spot where I had left Gan Had and Tun Gan. I was trying to figure how we might return to Morbus more quickly than we had come; but I knew that it would be difficult to better our speed, and I had to resign myself to the fact that it would be two days before I could reach the City, and in the meantime what might not have happened to Janai? I shuddered as I contemplated her fate; and I had to content myself with the reflection that if I could not rescue her, I might at least avenge her. I hated to think of forcing Tun Gan and Gan Had to return with me; but there was no other way. I needed the strength of their paddles to hasten my return. I could not even offer them the alternative of remaining on the island. Such were my thoughts as I came to the place where I had left the boat. It was gone. Gan Had and Tun Gan had deserted me, taking with them my only means of transportation back to Morbus.

For a moment I was absolutely stunned by the enormity of the misfortune that had overtaken me, for it seemed to preclude any possibility of my being able to be of any assistance whatever to Janai, for after all it was she alone who mattered. I sat down on the edge of the canal and sunk my face in my palms in a seemingly futile effort to plan for the future. I conceived and discarded a dozen mad projects, at last deciding upon the only one which seemed to offer any chance of success. I determined to return to the camp of the hormads and give myself up. At least then I could be near Janai, and once back in Morbus with her some fortunate circumstance might give me the opportunity that I sought, though my better judgment told me that death would be my only reward.

I arose then, and started boldly back toward the camp; but as I approached it, and before I was discovered, another plan occurred to me. Were I to return to Morbus as a prisoner, bound hand and foot, Ay-mad would doubtless have me destroyed while I was still helpless, for he knew my great strength and feared it; but if I could reach Morbus undiscovered I might accomplish something more worthwhile; and if I could reach it before Janai was returned to Ay-mad, my chances of saving her from him would be increased a thousandfold; so now I moved more cautiously circling the camp until I came upon the malagors, some resting in sleep, their heads tucked beneath their giant wings, while others moved restlessly about. They were not tethered in any way, for the hormads knew that they would not take flight after dark of their own volition.

Circling still farther, I approached them from the far side of the camp; and as I was a hormad, I aroused no suspicion among them. Walking up to the first one I encountered, I took hold of its neck and led it quietly away; and when I felt that I was far enough away from camp for safety, I leaped to its back. I knew how to control the great bird, as I had watched Teeaytan-ov carefully at the time that I was captured and transported from the vicinity of Phundahl to Morbus; and I had often talked with both officers and hormad warriors about them, thus acquiring all the knowledge that was necessary to control and direct them.

At first the bird objected to taking off and endeavored to fight me, so that I was afraid the noise would attract attention from the camp; and presently it did, for I heard someone shout, "What is going on out there?" And presently, in the light of the farther moon, I saw three hormads approaching.

Once more I sought to urge the great bird to rise, kicking

it violently with my heels. Now the hormads were running toward me, and the whole camp was aroused. The bird, excited by my buffetings and by the noise of the warriors approaching behind us, commenced to run away from them; and spreading its great wings, it flapped them vigorously for a moment; and then we rose from the ground and sailed off into the night.

By the stars, I headed it for Morbus; and that was all that I had to do, for its homing instinct kept it thereafter upon the right course.

The flight was rapid and certain, though the malagor became excited when Thuria leaped from below the horizon and hurtled through the sky.

Thuria, less than six thousand miles from the surface of Barsoom, and circling the planet in less than eight hours, presents a magnificent spectacle as it races through the heavens, a spectacle well calculated to instill terror in the hearts of lower animals whose habits are wholly diurnal. However my bird held its direction, though it flew very low as if it were trying to keep as far away as possible from the giant ball of fire that appeared to be pursuing it.

Ah, our Martian nights! A gorgeous spectacle that never ceases to enthrall the imagination of Barsoomians. How pale and bleak must seem the nights on earth, with a single satellite moving at a snail's pace through the sky at such a great distance from the planet that it must appear no larger than a platter Even with the stress under which my mind was laboring, I still could thrill to the magnificent spectacle of this glorious night.

The distance that had required two days and nights of arduous efforts in coming from Morbus was spanned in a few hours by the swift malagor. It was with some difficulty that I forced the creature down upon the island from which we had set forth two days before, as it wished to land in its accustomed place before the gates of Morbus; but at last I succeeded, and it was with a sigh of relief that I slipped from the back of my unwilling mount.

It did not want to take off again, but I forced it to do so, as I could not afford to take the chance that it might be seen if it arose from the island after sunrise, and thus lead my enemies to my only sanctuary when their suspicions were aroused by the tale which I knew the returning searching party would have to tell.

After I had succeeded in chasing it away, I went immediately to the mouth of the tunnel leading back to the Laboratory Building, where I removed enough debris to permit me to crawl through into the tunnel. Before doing so, I tore up a large bush and as I wormed myself backward through the aperture I drew the bush after me, in the hope that it would fill the hole and conceal the opening. Then I hurried through the long tunnel to 3—17.

It was with a feeling of great relief that I found my body still safe in its vault-like tomb. For a moment I stood looking down at it, and I think that with the exception of Janai I had never so longed to possess any other thing. My face and my body may have their faults, but by comparison with the grotesque monstrosity that my brain now directed, they were among the most beautiful things in the world; but there they lay, as lost to me as completely as though they had gone to the incinerator unless Ras Thavas should return.

Ras Thavas! John Carter! Where were they? Perhaps slain in Phundahl; perhaps long since killed by the Great Toonolian Marshes; perhaps the victims of some accident on their return journey to Helium, if they had succeeded in reaching John Carter's flier outside Phundahl. I had practically given up hope that they would return for me, because enough time had elapsed to permit John Carter to have made the trip to Helium and to have returned easily, long before this; yet hope would not die.

CHAPTER XX

THE MIGHTY JED OF GOOLIE

I REALIZED THAT MY plans from now on must depend upon the conditions which confronted me. My hope was that I might reach the palace of Ay-mad, undetected, and hide myself in the throne room until Janai was brought before him. I should then attempt to destroy Ay-mad, and if I succeeded, which I had no doubt but that I should, to fight my way with Janai toward liberty. That I should fail seemed quite probable; but at least I should have destroyed her worst enemy, and might even find sufficient following among the hormads, which were always discontented with their rulers, to promise some success in taking over the city and Island of Morbus. This was my dream; but it was doomed never to be realized. I had been reckoning without consideration of Vat Room No. 4.

As I approached the door that opened into the corridor, I thought that I heard sounds beyond the heavy panels; so that it was with the utmost caution that I opened the doors gradually. As I did so, the sound came more plainly to my ears. It was indescribable—a strange surging sound, unlike any other sound in the world, and blending with it were strange human voices mouthing unintelligibly.

Even before I looked out, I knew then what it was; and as I stepped into the corridor I saw at my right and not far from the door a billowing mass of slimy, human tissue creeping gradually toward me. Protruding from it were unrelated fragments of human anatomy—a hand, an entire leg, a foot, a lung, a heart, and here and there a horribly mouthing head. The heads screamed at me, and a hand tried to reach forth and clutch me; but I was well without their reach. Had I arrived an hour later, and opened that door, the whole horrid mass would have surged in upon me and the body of Vor Daj would have been lost forever.

The corridor to the left, leading to the ramp that led to the upper floors, was quite deserted. I realized that the mass in Vat Room No. 4 must have found entrance at the far end of the pits through some unguarded opening below the street level. Eventually it would fill every crevice and make its way up the ramp to the upper stories of the Laboratory Building.

What, I wondered, would be the end? Theoretically, it would never cease to grow and spread unless entirely destroyed. It would spread out of the City of Morbus and across the Great Toonolian Marshes. It would engulf cities; or failing to mount their walls, it would surround and isolate them, condemning their inhabitants to slow starvation. It would roll across the dead sea bottoms to the farmlands of Mars' great canals. Eventually it would cover the entire surface of the planet, destroying all other life. Conceivably, it might grow and grow through all eternity devouring and living upon itself. It was a hideous thing to contemplate, but it was not without probability. Ras Thavas himself had told me as much.

I hastened along the corridor toward the ramp, expecting that I would probably find no other abroad at this time of night, as the discipline and guarding of the Laboratory Building was extremely lax when left to the direction of the hormads, as it had been after I had been demoted; but to my chagrin and consternation I found the upper floors alive with warriors and officers. A veritable panic reigned, and to such an extent that no one paid any attention to me. The officers were trying to maintain some form of order and discipline; but they were failing signally in the face of the terror that was apparent everywhere. From snatches of conversation which I overheard, I learned that the mass from Vat Room No. 4 had entered the palace and that Ay-mad and his court were fleeing to another part of the island outside the city walls. I learned, too, that the mass was spreading through the avenues of the city, and the fear of the hormad warriors was that they would all be cut off from escape. Ay-mad had issued orders that they should remain and attempt to destroy the mass and prevent its further spread through the city. Some of the officers were half-heartedly attempting to enforce the order, but for the most part they were as anxious to flee as the common warriors themselves.

Suddenly one warrior raised his voice above the tumult and shouted to his fellows. "Why should we remain here to die, while Ay-mad escapes with his favorites? There is still one avenue open; come, follow me!"

That was enough. Like a huge wave, the hideous monsters swept the officers to one side, killing some and trampling others, as they bolted for the exit which led to the only avenue of escape left open to them. Nothing could withstand them, and I was carried along in the mad rush for safety.

It was just as well, for if Ay-mad was leaving the City, Janai would not be brought into it.

Once in the avenue, the congestion was relieved, and we moved along in a steady stream toward the outer gate; but the flight did not stop here, as the terrified hormads spread over the Island in an attempt to get as far away from the City as possible; so I found myself standing almost alone in the open space before the City where the malagors landed and from which they took off in their flight. To this spot would the captors of Janai bring her; so here I would remain hoping that some fortunate circumstance might suggest a plan whereby I might rescue her from this city of horrors.

It seemed that I had never before had to wait so long for dawn, and I found myself almost alone on the stretch of open plain that lay between the City gates and the shore of the lake. A few officers and warriors remained at the gate, and scouts were continually entering the City and reporting back the progress of the mass. I thought that they had not noticed me, but presently one of the officers approached me.

"What are you doing here?" he demanded.

"I was sent here by Ay-mad," I replied.

"Your face is very familiar," said the officer. "I am sure that I have seen you before. Something about you arouses my suspicions."

I shrugged. "It does not make much difference," I said, "what you think. I am Ay-mad's messenger, and I carry orders for the officer in command of the party that went in search of the fugitives."

"Oh," he said, "that is possible; still I feel that I know you."

"I doubt it," I replied. "Ever since I was created, I have lived in a small village at the end of the island."

"Perhaps so," he said. "It doesn't make any difference, anyway. What message do you bring to the commander of the search party?"

"I have orders for the commander of the gate, also."

"I am he," said the officer.

"Good," I replied. "My orders are to take the woman, if she has been recaptured, upon a malagor and fly her directly to Ay-mad, and the captain of the gate is made responsible to see that this is done. I feel sorry for you, if there is any hitch."

"There will be no hitch," he said; "but I do not see why there should be."

"There may be, though," I assured him, "for some informer has told Ay-mad that the commander of the search party wishes Janai for himself. In all the confusion and insubordination and mutiny that has followed the abandonment of the city, Ay-mad is none too sure of himself or his power; so he is fearful that this officer may take advantage of conditions to defy him and keep the girl for himself when he learns what has happened here during his absence."

"Well," said the captain of the gate, "I'll see to that."

"It might be well," I suggested, "not to let the officer in command of the party know what you have in mind. I will hide inside the city gates so that he will not see me; and you can bring the girl to me and, later, a malagor, while you engage the officer in conversation and distract his attention. Then, when I have flown away, you may tell him."

"That is a good idea," he said. "You are not such a fool as you look."

"I am sure," I said, "that you will find you have made no mistake in your estimate of me."

"Look!" he said, "I believe they are coming now." And

sure enough, far away, and high in the sky, a little cluster of dots were visible which grew rapidly larger and larger, resolving themselves finally into eleven malagors with their burdens of warriors and captives.

As the party came closer and prepared to land, I stepped inside the gate where I could not be observed or recognized by any of them. The captain of the gate advanced and greeted the commander of the returning search party. They spoke briefly for a few moments, and then I saw Janai coming toward the gate; and presently a warrior followed her, leading a large malagor. I scrutinized the fellow carefully as he approached; but I did not recognize him, and so I was sure that he would not know me, and then Janai entered and stood face to face with me.

"Tor-dur-bar." she exclaimed.

"Quiet," I whispered. "You are in grave danger from which I think I can save you if you will trust me, as evidently you have not in the past."

"I have not known whom to trust," she said, "but I have trusted you more than any other."

The warrior had now reached the gate with the malagor. I tossed Janai to its back and leaped astride the great bird behind her; then we were off. I directed the flight of the bird toward the east end of the island, to make them think I was taking Janai to Ay-mad; but when we had crossed some low hills and they were hidden from my view, I turned back around the south side of the island and headed toward Phundahl.

As we started to fly from the island the great bird became almost unmanageable, trying to return again to its fellows. I had to fight it constantly to keep it headed in the direction I wished to travel. These exertions coming upon top of its long flight tired it rapidly so that eventually it gave up and flapped slowly and dismally along the route I had chosen. Then, for the first time, Janai and I were able to converse.

"How did you happen to be at the gate when I arrived?" she asked. "How is it that you are the messenger whom Ay-mad chose to bring me to him?"

"Ay-mad knows nothing about it," I replied. "It is all a little fiction of my own which I invented to deceive the captain of the gate and the commander of the party that recaptured you."

"But how did you know that I had been recaptured and that I would be returned to Morbus today? It is all very confusing and baffling; I cannot understand it."

"Did you not hear that a malagor was stolen from your camp last night?" I asked.

"Tor-dur-bar!" she exclaimed. "It was you? What were you doing there?"

"I had set out in search of you and was beside the island when your party landed."

"I see," she said. "How very clever and how very brave."

"If you had believed in me and trusted me," I said, "we might have escaped; but I do not believe that I would have been such a fool as to be recaptured, as was Sytor."

"I believed in you and trusted you more than any other," she said.

"Then why did you run away with Sytor?" I demanded.

"I did not run away with Sytor. He tried to persuade me, telling me many stories about you which I did not wish to believe. Finally I told him definitely that I would not go with him, but he and Pandar came in the night and took me by force."

"I am glad that you did not go away with him willingly," I said. I can tell you that it made me feel very good to think that she had not done so; and now I loved her more than ever, but little good it would do me as long as I sported this hideous carcass and monstrously inhuman face.

"And what of Vor Daj?" she asked presently.

"We shall have to leave his body where it is until Ras Thavas returns; there is no alternative."

"But if Ras Thavas never returns?" she asked, her voice trembling.

"Then Vor Daj will lie where he is through all eternity," I replied.

"How horrible," she breathed. "He was so handsome, so wonderful."

"You thought well of him?" I asked. And I was immediately ashamed of myself for taking this unfair advantage of her.

"I thought well of him," she said, in a matter-of-fact tone, a reply which was neither very exciting nor very encouraging. She might have spoken in the same way of a thoat or a calot.

Sometime after noon, it became apparent that the malagor had about reached the limit of its endurance. It began to drop closer and closer toward the marshes, and presently it came to the ground upon one of the largest islands that I had seen. It was a very attractive island, with hill and dale and forest land, and a little stream winding down to the lake, a most unusual sight upon Barsoom. The moment that the malagor alighted, it rolled over upon its side throwing us to the ground, and I thought that it was about to die as it lay there struggling and gasping.

"Poor thing!" said Janai "It has been carrying double for three days now, and with insufficient food, practically none at all."

"Well, it has at least brought us away from Morbus," I said, "and if it recovers it is going to take us on to Helium."

"Why to Helium?" she asked.

"Because it is the only country where I am sure you will find safe asylum."

"And why should I find safety there?" she demanded.

"Because you are a friend of Vor Daj; and John Carter, Warlord of Barsoom, will see that any friend of Vor Daj is well received and well treated."

"And you?" she asked. I must have shuddered visibly at the thought of entering Helium in this horrible guise, for she said quickly, "I am sure that you will be received well, too, for you certainly deserve it far more than I" She thought for a moment in silence, and then she asked, "Do you know what became of the brain of Vor Daj? Sytor told me that it was destroyed."

I wanted to tell her the truth; but I could not bring myself to it, and so I said, "It was not destroyed Ras Thavas knows where it is; and if I ever find him, it will be restored to Vor Daj."

"It does not seem possible that we two shall ever find Ras Thavas," she said, sadly.

It did not seem likely to me either, but I would not give up hope. John Carter must live! Ras Thavas must live! And some day I should find them.

But what of my body lying there beneath the Laboratory Building of Morbus? What if the mass from Vat Room No. 4 found its way into 3—17? The very thought made me feel faint; and yet it was not impossible. If the building and the corridor filled with the mass, the great pressure that it would exert might conceivably break down even the massive door of 3—17. Then those horrid heads would devour me, or, if the mass spread from the Island across the marshes, it would be impossible ever to retrieve my body even though it remained forever untouched. It was not a very cheerful outlook, and I found it extremely depressing; but my thoughts were suddenly recalled to other channels by an exclamation from Janai.

"Look!" she cried.

I turned in the direction she was pointing, to see a number

of strange creatures coming toward us in prodigious leaps and bounds. That they were some species of human being was apparent, but there were variations which rendered them unlike any other animal on Mars. They had long, powerful legs, the knees of which were always flexed except immediately after the take-off of one of their prodigious leaps, and they had long, powerful tails; otherwise, they seemed quite human in conformation. As they came closer, I noted that they were entirely naked except for a simple harness which supported a short sword on one side and a dagger on the other. Besides these weapons, each of them carried a spear in his right hand. They quickly surrounded us, remaining at a little distance from us, squatting down with their knees bent as they supported themselves on their broad, flat feet and their tails.

"Who are you, and what are you doing here?" demanded one of them, surprising me by the fact that he possessed speech.

"We were flying over your island," I replied, when our malagor became tired and was forced to come to ground to rest. As soon as we are able, we shall continue on our way."

The fellow shook his head. "You will never leave Gooli," he said. He was examining me closely. "What are you?" he asked.

"I am a man," I said, stretching the point a little.

He shook his head. "And what is that?" He pointed at Janai.

"A woman," I replied.

Again he shook his head.

"She is only half a woman," he said. "She has no way of rearing her young or keeping them warm. If she had any, they would die as soon as they were hatched."

Well, that was a subject I saw no reason for going into, and so I kept silent. Janai seemed slightly amused, for if she were nothing else she was extremely feminine.

"What do you intend to do with us?" I demanded.

"We shall take you to the Jed, and he will decide. Perhaps he will let you live and work; perhaps he will destroy you. You are very ugly, but you look strong; you should be a good worker. The woman appears useless, if she can be called a woman."

I was at a loss as to what to do. We were surrounded by fully fifty warriors, well though crudely armed. With my terrific strength, I might have destroyed many of them; but eventually I was sure that they would overpower and kill me.

It would be better to go with them to their Jed and await a better opportunity for escape. "Very well," I said, "we will go with you."

"Of course you will," he said. "What else could you do?"

"I could fight," I said.

"Ho ho, you would like to fight, would you?" he demanded. "Well, I think that if that is the case, the Jed will accommodate you. Come with us."

They led us back along the stream and up over a little rise of ground beyond which we saw a forest, at the edge of which lay a village of thatched huts.

"That," said the leader, pointing, "is Gooli, the largest city in the world. There, in his great palace, dwells Anatok, Jed of Gooli and all of the Island of Ompt."

As we approached the village, a couple of hundred people came to meet us. There were men, women and children; and when I examined the women I realized why the leader of the party that had captured us thought that Janai was not wholly feminine. These Goolians of the Island of Ompt are marsupials, oviparous marsupials. The females lay eggs which they carry in a pouch on the lower part of their abdomen. In this pouch the eggs hatch, and in it the young live and take shelter until they are able to fend for themselves. It was quite amusing to see the little heads protruding from their mothers' pouches as they surveyed us with wondering eyes. Up to this time I had believed that there was only one marsupial upon Barsoom, and that a reptile, so it seemed quite remarkable to see these seemingly quite human people bearing their young in abdominal pouches

The creatures that came out from the village to meet us were quite rough with us, pulling and hauling us this way and that as they sought to examine us more closely. I towered above them all and they were a little in awe of me; but they were manhandling Janai quite badly when I interfered, pushing several of them away so forcibly that they were thrown to the ground, whereupon two or three of them drew their swords and came for me; but the party that had captured us acted now as a bodyguard and defended us from attack. After this they kept the rabble at a distance, and presently we were ushered into the village and led to a grass hut much larger than the others. This, I assumed, was the magnificent palace of Anatok. Such it proved to be, and presently the Jed himself emerged from the interior with several men and women and a horde of children. The women were his wives and their attendants, the men were his counselors.

Anatok seemed much interested in us and asked many questions about our capture, and then he asked us from whence we came.

"We came from Morbus," I said, "and we are on our way to Helium."

"Morbus—Helium," he repeated. "I never heard of them. Little villages, no doubt, inhabited by savages. How fortunate we are to live in such a splendid city as Gooli. Don't you think so?" he asked.

"I think you would be very much happier in Gooli than in Morbus, and far more at ease here than in Helium," I replied, truthfully.

"Our countries," I continued, "have never harmed you. We are not at war; therefore you should let us go on our way in peace."

At that he laughed. "What simple people come from other villages!" he exclaimed. "You are my slaves. When you are no longer of service to me you shall be destroyed. Do you think that we want any strangers to go away from Ompt to lead enemies here to destroy our magnificent city and steal our vast riches?"

"Our people would never bother you," I said. "Our country is too far from here. If one of your people should come to our country, he would be treated with kindness. We fight only with our enemies."

"That reminds me," said the leader of the party that had captured us, "this fellow is indeed our enemy by his own words, for he said that he wished to fight us."

"What!" exclaimed Anatok. "Well, if that is so, he shall have his wish. There is nothing that we like better than a good fight. With what weapons would you like to fight?"

"I will fight with anything that my antagonist chooses," I replied.

CHAPTER XXI

DUEL TO THE DEATH

IT SOON APPEARED that a personal combat was a matter of considerable importance to the Goolians. The chief and his advisors held a lengthy discussion relative to the selection of an antagonist for me. The qualities of a number of warriors were discussed, and even their ancestors as far back as the fifth and sixth generation were appraised and compared. It might have been a momentous matter of state, so serious were they. The conference was often interrupted by suggestions and comments from other members of the tribe; but at last they selected a husky young buck, who, impressed by the importance now attached to him, launched into a long and windy speech in which he enumerated his many virtues and those of his ancestors while belittling me and bragging about the short work he would make of me. He finally concluded his harangue by selecting swords as the weapons we were to use; and then Anatok asked me if I had anything to say, for it seemed that this speech-making was a part of the ceremony preceding the duel.

"I have only a question to ask," I replied.

"And what is that?" demanded Anatok.

"What will be my reward if I defeat your warrior?" I asked.

Anatok appeared momentarily confused. "Now that is an outcome that had not occurred to me," he said; "but of course, after all, it is unimportant, as you will not win."

"But it might happen," I insisted, "and if it does, what is to be my reward? Will you grant freedom to my companion and myself?"

Anatok laughed. "Certainly," he said. "I can safely promise you anything you ask for; for when the fight is over you will have lost, and you will be dead."

"Very good," I replied; "but don't forget your promise."

"Is that all you have to say?" demanded Anatok. "Aren't you going to tell us how good you are, and how many men you have killed, and what a wonderful fighter you are? Or aren't you any good?"

"That is something that only the sword may decide," I replied. "My antagonist has done a great deal of boasting, and he might continue to do so indefinitely without drawing any blood or harming me in any way. He has not even frightened me, for I have heard men boast before; and those who boasted the loudest usually have the least to boast about."

"It is evident," said Anatok, "that you know nothing about the warriors of Gooli. We are the bravest people in the world and our warriors are the greatest swordsmen. It is because of these attributes that we are the most powerful nation in the world, which is evidenced by the fact that we have built this magnificent city and protected it for generations, and that we have been able during all this time to safeguard our vast treasures."

I looked around at the mean little village of grass huts and wondered where Anatok's vast treasures might be hidden, and of what they consisted. Perhaps it was a vast store of rare gems and precious metals.

"I see no evidence of great wealth or of any treasure," I said. "Perhaps you are only boasting again."

At this, Anatok flew into a rage. "You dare doubt me, you hideous savage?" he cried. "What do you know of wealth or treasures? Your eyes have probably never rested upon anything that compares with the riches of Gooli."

"Show him the treasure before he dies," cried a warrior. "Then he will understand why we have to be such a brave and warlike people in order to protect and hold it."

"That is not a bad idea," said Anatok. "Let him learn by his own eyes that we of Gooli do not boast about our wealth, just as he will learn by experience that we do not boast about our bravery and swordsmanship. Come, fellow, you shall see the treasures."

He led the way into his palace, and I followed with a score of warriors pressing about me. The interior of the grass hut was bare, except for a litter of dead grass and leaves around the walls which evidently served for beds, some weapons, a few crude cooking utensils, and a large chest that stood in the exact center of the building. To this chest, Anatok conducted me; and, with a grand flourish, raised the lid and exhibited the contents to me as much as to say, "Now there is nothing more in the world for you to see; you have seen everything."

"Here," he said, "are the riches of Gooli."

The chest was about three-quarters filled with marine shells. Anatok and the others watched me closely to note my reaction.

"Where is the treasure?" I asked. "These are nothing but shells."

Anatok trembled with suppressed rage. "You poor, ignorant savage," he cried. "I might have known that you could not appreciate the true value and beauty of the treasure of Gooli. Come, on with the fight; the sooner you are destroyed, the better off the world will be. We Goolians cannot abide ignorance and stupidity; we, who are the most intelligent and wisest people in the world."

"Come on," I said. "The quicker we get it over the better."

It appeared that the preparation for the duel was quite a ceremonious affair. A procession was formed with Anatok and his counselors at the head. Then, following my antagonist, was a guard of honor consisting of about ten warriors. Behind these, I trailed; and would have been alone but for the fact that I took Janai with me, nor did they raise any objections to this. The rest of the tribe, including warriors, women and children, followed behind us. It was a remarkable procession in that it was all procession and no audience. We marched around the palace once and then down the main street and out of the village. The villagers formed a circle, in the center of which were I, my antagonist and his guard of honor. At a word from Anatok I drew my sword; so did my antagonist and the ten warriors with him. Then we advanced toward one another.

I turned to Anatok. "What are those other warriors doing there?" I asked.

"They are Zuki's assistants," he replied.

"Am I supposed to fight all of them?" I demanded.

"Oh, no," replied Anatok. "You will only fight Zuki, and his assistants will only help him if he gets in trouble."

In reality then, I was to fight eleven men.

"Fight, coward!" cried Anatok. "We want to see a good fight."

I turned again toward Zuki and his helpers. They were coming toward me very, very slowly; and they were making faces at me as though in an effort to frighten me. The whole thing struck me as so ridiculous that I could not refrain from laughing; yet I knew that it was serious, for the odds of eleven to one were heavily against me, even though the eleven might be inferior swordsmen.

My face was in itself extremely hideous, and suddenly I twisted it into a horrible grimace and with a wild shout leaped toward them. The reaction was amazing. Zuki was the first to turn and flee, colliding with his fellows, who, in their turn, attempted to escape my onslaught. I did not pursue them; and when they saw that I had not, they stopped and faced me again.

"Is this an example of the vaunted courage of the Goolis?" I asked Anatok.

"You have just witnessed a fine piece of strategy," replied Anatok; "but you are too ignorant to appreciate it."

Once again they came toward me, but still very slowly; and this time they voiced a kind of war whoop while they were making their faces.

I was just about to rush them again when a woman screamed and pointed down the valley. With the others, I turned to see what had attracted her attention, and discovered half a dozen savages such as those which had attacked our boat while Gan Had, Tun Gan, and I had been pursuing Sytor and Janai. At sight of them, a great wail rose from the villagers. The women and children and all but a handful of warriors ran for the woods; and I couldn't tell whether those who remained did so because they were paralyzed with fright and unable to run, or because of a sudden access of courage. Zuki, my late antagonist, was not among them. He and Anatok were racing nip and tuck for the woods in advance of all the others.

"Who are they?" I asked a warrior standing near me.

"The man-eaters," he replied. "After their last raid, we were chosen to be the sacrifice when they should come again."

"What do you mean," I asked, " 'the sacrifice?' "

"Yes, it is a sacrifice," he replied. "If we do not willingly give up five warriors to them when they come, they will attack the village and burn it, they will take our treasure, they will steal our women and kill as many of our men as they can find. It is simpler this way; but it is hard on those who are chosen. However, we have no alternative but to obey, for if we did not the tribe would kill us with torture."

"But why give up to them?" I asked. "There are only six, and we are six; let's fight them. We have as good a chance to win as they."

They looked at me in surprise. "But we never fight anyone," they said, "unless we outnumber them ten to one. It would not be good strategy."

"Forget your strategy," I commanded, "and stand up against these men with me."

"Do you suppose we could?" asked one of another.

"It has never been done," was the reply.

"That is no reason why it can't be done now," I snapped. "If you will give me even a little help, we can kill them all."

"Give me a sword," said Janai, "and I will help, too."

"Let us try it," said one of the Goolians.

"Why not?" demanded another. "We are going to die anyway."

The savages had now approached and were quite near us. They were laughing and talking among themselves and casting contemptuous glances at the Goolians. "Come on," said one, "throw down your arms and come with us."

117

For answer, I leaped forward and clove the fellow from crown to breastbone with a single stroke. The five Goolians came forward slowly. They had no stomach for fighting; but when they saw the success of my first blow they were encouraged; and, in the same measure, the savages were taken aback. I did not stop with the one but pushed on toward the remainder of the savages. I now met with a little competition; but my great reach and my enormous strength gave me an advantage which they could not overcome, with the result that three of them were soon down and the other three running away as fast as they could go.

At sight of the enemy in retreat, something which they had probably seldom seen in their lives, the Goolians became demons of bravery and set out in pursuit of them. They could easily have overtaken them, for they moved in great bounds that carried them fully twenty feet at a time; but they let them escape over the edge of the plateau; and then they came bounding back, their chests stuck out and their expressions radiating self-satisfaction and egotism.

Evidently the encounter had been witnessed by those in hiding in the woods, for now the entire tribe came straggling toward us. Anatok looked a little shame-faced, but his first words belied his expression. "You see the value of our strategy," he said. "By appearing to run away in fright, we lured them on and then destroyed them."

"You are not fooling me or yourself either," I said. "You are a race of braggarts and cowards. I saved the five men that you would have given up as tribute without a single effort to defend them. You permitted six savages to route you and all your warriors. I could kill you all single-handed, and you know it. Now I demand that you reward me for what I have done by permitting me and my companion to remain here in safety until we are able to make plans for continuing our journey. If you refuse, you shall be the first to feel the edge of my sword."

"You don't have to threaten me," he said, trembling. "It was my intention to give you your liberty as a reward for what you have done. You are free to remain with us and to go and come as you please. You may remain as long as you like, if you will fight against our enemies when they come."

CHAPTER XXII

OFF FOR PHUNDAHL

THE NEXT DAY Janai and I went to look for our malagor to see if he had recovered; but we could find no trace of him; so I assumed that he had either flown away or been seized by the savages, who, Anatok told me, came from another island some distance from Gooli.

I immediately set to work building a boat, and in this the Goolians helped me a little although they were extremely lazy and tired easily. They were without doubt the most useless race of people I had ever encountered, expending practically all their energies in boasting and little or none in accomplishment. Within a few hours after the encounter with the savages, they were boasting of their great victory and taking all the credit to themselves, Anatok claiming most of it for his marvelous strategy, as he called it. There are lots of people in the world like the Goolians, but some of them are never found out.

I became quite intimate with Zuki in the weeks that followed while we were building the boat. I found him rather above average intelligence and the possessor of a rudimentary sense of humor which the other Goolians seemed to lack entirely. One day I asked him why they considered the shells such a valuable treasure.

"Anatok has to have the treasure," he replied, "in order to give him a feeling of superiority; and it was the same way with the rulers who preceded him, and, in fact, with all of us. It makes us feel tremendously important to have a great treasure; but, being a cautious people, we chose a treasure that nobody else would want; otherwise, warlike people would be coming constantly to steal our treasure from us. Sometimes I think it is a little silly, but I would not dare say so to Anatok or to any others. All their lives they have heard of the great value of the vast treasure of Gooli; and so they have come to believe in it, and they do not question it because they do not wish to question it."

"And they feel the same way about their vaunted courage and the strategy of Anatok?" I asked.

"Oh, that is different," replied Zuki. "Those things are

real. We are really the bravest people in the world, and Anatok the greatest strategist."

Well, his sense of humor had gone the limit in questioning the treasure. It couldn't stand the strain of doubting the valor of the Goolis or the strategy of Anatok. Perhaps the Goolis were better off as they were, for their silly egotism gave them a certain morale that would have been wholly lacking had they admitted the truth.

Janai worked with me in the building of the boat, and so we were much together; but I always had the feeling that I was repulsive to her. She never touched me, if she could avoid it; nor did she often look directly at my face, nor could I blame her; yet I was sure that she was becoming fond of me as one becomes fond of an ugly but faithful dog. It made me wish that I really were a dog, for at least then she would have caressed me; but I was so much uglier than even a calot of Mars that I should always be repulsive to her no matter how kindly she might feel toward me.

These thoughts made me wonder about my poor body. Was it still safely hidden in 3–17, or had the door burst open and the horrid mass from Vat Room No. 4 engulfed and devoured it? Would I ever see it again? Would I ever again possess it, and animate it with this brain of mine which existed solely for Janai without her ever being aware of it? It all seemed very hopeless, and now that we had lost our malagor the trip to Helium seemed little short of an impossibility of accomplishment.

At last the boat was completed, and the Goolians helped me to carry it down to the lake. They stocked it with provisions for me, and they gave me extra spears and a sword and dagger for Janai. They bragged about the building of the boat, telling us that it was the best boat that was ever built and that no one but Goolians could have built it. They bragged about the weapons they gave us and the provisions. Thus we left them still boasting, and set out upon our perilous journey toward the west through the Great Toonolian Marshes.

CHAPTER XXIII

CAPTIVES OF AMHOR

VAST EXPANSES OF the Great Marshes were uninhabitable by man, and for a week we passed through dismal wastes where not even the savage aborigines could live; but we encountered other menaces in the form of great reptiles and gigantic insects, some of the latter being of enormous proportions with a wing-spread well over thirty feet. Equipped with powerful jaws and rapier-like stingers, and sometimes with both, as some of them were, one of these monsters could easily have annihilated us; but fortunately we were never attacked. The smaller reptiles of the Marshes were their natural prey and we witnessed many an encounter in which the insects always came off victorious.

A week after we left Gooli we were paddling one day across one of the numerous lakes that dot the Marshes when, low above the horizon ahead of us, we saw a great battleship moving slowly in our direction. Instantly my heart leaped with joy.

"John Carter!" I cried. "He has come at last. Janai, you are saved."

"And Ras Thavas will be with him," she said, "and we can go back to Morbus and resurrect the body of Vor Daj."

"Once again he will live, and move, and love," I said, carried away by the relief and happiness which this anticipation engendered.

"But suppose it is not John Carter?" she asked.

"It must be, Janai, for what other civilized man would be cruising above this hideous waste?"

We stopped paddling and watched the great airship approach. It was cruising very low, scarcely a hundred feet above the ground and moving quite slowly. As it came nearer, I stood up in the canoe and waved to attract attention, even though I knew that they could not fail to see us for they were coming directly toward us.

The ship bore no insignia to proclaim its nationality, but this is not unusual in Martian navies where a lone vessel is entering into potential enemy country. The lines of the ship, too, were quite unfamiliar to me; that is, I could not identify the vessel. It was evidently one of the older ships of the line, many of which were still in commission on the frontiers of Helium. I could not understand why John Carter had chosen such a craft in preference to one of the swift, new types; but I knew that he must have a very good reason which it was not mine to question.

As the ship drew nearer it dropped still lower; so I knew that we had been observed; and finally it came to rest just above us. Landing tackle was lowered to us through a keel port, and I quickly made it fast to Janai's body so that she could be raised comfortably to the ship. While I was engaged in this, another tackle was lowered for me; and soon we were both being hoisted toward the vessel.

The instant that we were hoisted into the hold of the vessel, and I had a chance to note the sailors who surrounded us, I realized that this was no ship of Helium for the men wore the harness of another country.

Janai turned toward me with frightened eyes "Neither John Carter nor Ras Thavas are on this ship," she whispered; "it is no ship of Helium, but one of the ships of Jal Had, Prince of Amhor I should have been as well off in Morbus as I shall be now, if they discover my identity."

"You must not let them know," I said. "You are from Helium; remember that." She nodded in understanding.

The officers and sailors who surrounded us were far more interested in me than they were in Janai, commenting freely upon my hideousness.

We were immediately taken to the upper deck and before the officer in command. He looked at me in ill-disguised repugnance.

"Who are you?" he demanded. "And where do you come from?"

"I am a hormad from Morbus," I replied, "and my companion is a girl from Helium, a friend of John Carter, Warlord of Mars."

He looked at Janai long and earnestly for a moment. Then a nasty little smile touched his lips. "When did you change your nationality, Janai?" he asked. "You needn't attempt to deny your identity, Janai; I know you. I would know that face anywhere among millions, for your portrait hangs in my cabin as it hangs in the cabin of the commander of every ship of Amhor; and great is to be the reward of him who brings you back to Jal Had, the Prince."

"She is under the protection of the Warlord of Mars," I said. "No matter what reward Jal Had has offered you, John Carter will give you more if you return Janai to Helium."

"Who is this thing?" the commander demanded of Janai, nodding his head toward me. "Weren't you his prisoner?"

"No," she replied. "He is my friend. He has risked his life many times to save me, and he was trying to take me to Helium when you captured us. Please do not take me back to Amhor. I am sure that, if Tor-dur-bar says it is true, John Carter will pay you well if you bring us both to Helium."

"And be tortured to death by Jal Had when I get back to

122

Amhor?" demanded the commander. "No sir! Back to Amhor you go; and I shall probably get an extra reward when I deliver this freak to Jal Had. It will make a valuable addition to his collection, and greatly amuse and entertain the citizens of Amhor. If you behave yourself, Janai, you will be treated well by Jal Had. Do not be such a little fool as you were before. After all, it will not be so bad to be the Princess of Amhor."

"I would as lief mate with Ay-mad of Morbus," said the girl; "and sooner than that, I would die."

The commander shrugged. "That is your own affair," he said. "You will have plenty of time to think the matter over before we reach Amhor, and I advise you to think it over well and change your mind." He then gave instructions that quarters were to be assigned to us and that we were to be carefully watched but not confined if we behaved ourselves.

As we were being conducted toward a companionway that led below, I saw a man dart suddenly across the deck and leap overboard. He had done it so quickly that no one could intercept him; and though the commander had witnessed it no effort was made to save him, and the ship continued on its way. I asked the officer accompanying us who the man was and why he had leaped overboard.

"He was a prisoner who evidently preferred death to slavery in Amhor," he explained.

We were still very low above the surface of the lake, and one of the sailors who had run to the rail when the man had leaped overboard called back that the fellow was swimming toward our abandoned canoe.

"He won't last long in the Great Toonolian Marshes," commented the officer, as we descended toward our quarters.

Janai was given the best cabin on the boat; for they expected that she would be Princess of Amhor, and they wished to treat her well and curry her favor. I was relieved to know that at least until we reached Amhor she would be accorded every courtesy and consideration.

I was taken to a small cabin which accommodated two and was already occupied by another man. His back was toward me as I entered, as he was gazing out of a porthole. The officer closed the door behind me and departed, and I was left alone with my new companion. As the door slammed, he turned and faced me; and each of us voiced an exclamation of surprise. My roommate was Tun Gan. He looked a little frightened, when he recognized me, as his conscience must have been troubling him because of his desertion of me.

"So it is you?" I said.

"Yes, and I suppose you will want to kill me now," he replied; "but do not blame me too much. Pandar and I discussed it. We did not wish to desert you; but we knew that we should all die if we returned to Morbus, while if he and I went on in the canoe we at least might have a chance to escape."

"I do not blame you," I said. "Perhaps under identical circumstances I should have done the same thing. As it turned out, it was better that you deserted me, for because of it I was able to reach Morbus in a few hours and rescue Janai when she arrived with the party that had captured her; but how do you happen to be aboard this ship?"

"Pandar and I were captured about a week ago; and perhaps it was just as well, for we were being pursued by natives when this ship dropped down, frightening the natives away. We should doubtless have been captured and killed, otherwise; and I for one was glad to come aboard, but Pandar was not. He did not wish to go to Amhor, and slavery. All that he lived for was to get back to Phundahl."

"And where is Pandar now?" I asked.

"He just leaped overboard; I was watching him when you came in. He swam to the canoe, which I presume is the one you were taken from, and he is already paddling along on his way to Phundahl."

"I hope he reaches it," I said.

"He will not," prophesied Tun Gan. "I do not believe that any man alive can pass alone through the horrors of this hellish swamp."

"You have already come a long way," I reminded him.

"Yes, but who knows what lies ahead?"

"And you are not averse to going to Amhor?" I asked.

"Why should I be?" he asked, in turn. "They think I am Gantun Gur, the assassin of Amhor; and they treat me with great respect."

"Amazing!" I exclaimed. "For the moment I had forgotten that you had taken the body of Gantun Gur. Do you think that you can live up to it and continue to deceive them?"

"I think that I can," he replied. "My brain is not as dull as that of most hormads. I have told them that I received a head injury that has made me forget a great deal of my past life; and so far, they have not doubted me."

"They never will doubt you," I said; "because they cannot

conceive that the brain of another creature has been grafted into the skull of Gantun Gur."

"Then if you do not tell them, they will never know," he said, "for I certainly shall not tell them; so please remember to call me by my new name. What are you smiling at?"

"The situation is amusing. Neither one of us is himself. I have your body, and you have the body of another man."

"But who were you, whose brain is in my body?" he demanded. "I have often wondered about that."

"Continue to wonder," I replied; "for you may never know."

He looked at me keenly for a long moment. Suddenly his face brightened. "Now I know," he said. "How stupid of me not to have guessed before."

"You know nothing," I snapped; "and if I were you, I should not even guess."

He nodded. "Very well, Tor-dur-bar, it shall be as you wish."

To change the subject, I remarked, "I wonder what this ship from Amhor is doing sailing around alone over the Great Toonolian Marshes?"

"Jal Had, the Prince of Amhor, has a hobby for collecting wild beasts. They say that he has a great number of them, and this ship has been searching the Great Toonolian Marshes for new specimens."

"So they were not searching for Janai, then?"

"No. Was that Janai with you when you were captured? I got only a glimpse of two figures as our ship passed above you."

"Yes, Janai is aboard; and now I am faced with the problem of getting her off the ship before we reach Amhor."

"Well, perhaps you will be able to accomplish it," he said. "They ground the ship occasionally to hunt for new specimens, and the discipline is lax. As a matter of fact, they do not seem to guard us at all. That is why Pandar found it so easy to escape."

But no opportunity for escape was offered us, as the ship turned her nose directly for Amhor the moment that the commander realized that he had Janai aboard; nor did she once touch ground, nor again fly close to it.

Amhor lies about seven hundred and fifty earth miles directly north of the point at which our capture took place, which distance the ship covered in about seven and a half hours.

During this time I saw nothing of Janai, as she remained in her cabin.

We arrived above Amhor in the middle of the night, and we lay there floating above the city until morning, surrounded by patrol boats as a protection and guard for the precious cargo which we carried. Jal Had was asleep when we arrived, and no one had dared disturb him. I could tell by little things that I overheard that he had a sinister reputation and that everyone was very much afraid of him.

About the second zode a royal craft came along side and took Janai aboard, and I was helpless to prevent it; for they had removed me from Gantun Gur's cabin on our arrival above the city, and locked me in another one in the hold of the ship. I was filled with despondency, for I felt that now I should not only never regain my body, but never again see Janai. I did not care what became of me, and prayed only for death.

CHAPTER XXIV

CAGED

AFTER JANAI WAS taken from the ship, it was lowered to a landing stage and made fast; and shortly thereafter the door of my prison was opened, and I found myself confronted by a detachment of warriors in command of an officer. They carried heavy chains, and with these they manacled my hands. I did not resist, for I no longer cared.

I was then taken out onto the landing stage and, by elevator, to the ground. The warriors who had taken me from the ship were men who had not seen me before. They were very much interested in me, but seemed a little afraid. When we reached the avenue I attracted considerable attention, before I was hustled into a ground flier and whisked off down a broad avenue which led to the palace grounds.

These ground fliers are a common means of private transportation in many Martian cities. They have a ceiling of about one hundred feet and a maximum speed of sixty miles per hour. In Amhor all north and south traffic moves at ground level at intersections, east and west traffic passing above it. East and west traffic is compelled to rise above north and south traffic at each intersection because there is a short runway inclining upward to a height of about ten feet

126

at each intersection, ending in an abrupt drop at the intersection. These inclines force all east and west traffic to rise above the north and south traffic intersections. All vehicular traffic moves in but one direction on any avenue, the direction of flow alternating, so that half the avenues carry traffic in one direction and the other half in the opposite direction. Left turns are made without diminishing speed by the simple expedient of rising above both lanes of traffic. The result is that traffic flows steadily in all directions at an average speed of about fifty miles an hour. Parking accommodations are frequent, and are found inside buildings at a level of about sixty feet above the pavement. North and south pedestrian traffic moves without interruption in either direction on both sides of North and South Streets at the ground level; and, similarly, on East and West Streets through underpasses at street intersections.

I have gone into this matter of traffic control in a Martian city in some detail, and perhaps tediously, because of what John Carter has told me of the congestion and confusion in traffic handling in earthly cities, and in the hope that the inventors of our sister planet will be encouraged to develop ground fliers similar to those commonly used in the cities of Mars.

The palace grounds, which were our destination, covered an area of about eighty acres. The avenues leading to it were lined with the palaces of the nobility, just beyond which were the better-grade shops and hotels. Amhor is a small city and the only one in the principality which might claim the dignity of such a title, the others being but small and widely scattered villages. The chief business of the principality is the raising of thoats and zitidars, the former the saddle animals and the latter the mammoth draft animals of Mars. Both are also raised for food, and Amhor exports preserved meats, hides, and other by-products to Duhor, Phundahl, and Toonol.

Amhor is the mecca of the stockmen from the country, hard-riding, profane, belligerent men; good spenders, always provided with plenty of money. So it is withal an interesting city, though one may scarcely enjoy it from the inside of a cage in a zoological garden, which is exactly where I landed a few minutes after I was driven through the rear gate of the palace grounds.

Here, upon both sides of an avenue, were cages, pits, and dens containing specimens of a wide variety of Martian animal life, an exhibition of the fauna of a planet which must have been instructive and certainly was entertaining and amusing to the crowds that passed along the avenue daily; for to this part of the palace grounds the public was freely admitted during daylight hours.

A unique feature of the zoological display of Jal Had, Prince of Amhor, was the inclusion of various types of Martian humans. In the cage at my left was a huge green man, with his ivory tusks and four arms; and at my right was a red man from Ptarth. There were thoats and zitidars and the great white apes of Barsoom, fierce, hairy monsters closely resembling man, and, perhaps, the most feared of all Martian beasts. Near me also were two apts, artic monsters from far Okar. These great beasts are covered with white fur and have six legs, four of which are short and heavy and carry it over snow and ice. The other two grow forward from its shoulders on either side of its long, powerful neck, and terminate in white, hairless hands, with which it seizes and holds its prey. The head and mouth, John Carter has told me, are similar to those of an earthly hippopotamus, except that from the flat sides of the lower jawbone, two mighty horns curve slightly downward toward the front. Its two huge eyes extend in large oval patches from the center of the top of the cranium down either side of the head to below the roots of the horn, so that these weapons really grow out from the lower part of the eyes, which are composed of several thousand ocelli each. Each ocellus is furnished with its own lid, so that the apt can close as many of the facets of its eyes as it wishes. There were banths, calots, darseens, orluks, siths, soraks, ulsios and many other beasts, insects and men, including even a kaldane, one of the strange spider-men of Bantoom. But when they turned me into my cage, I immediately became the prize specimen of the exhibition. I must admit that I was by far the most hideous creature in the zoo. Perhaps in time I should have become proud of the distinction, for I attracted far more attention than even the most appalling of the horrid beasts that Jal Had had succeeded in collecting.

Gaping crowds stood in front of my cage, many of them poking sticks at me or throwing pebbles or bits of food. Presently an attendant came with a sign which I had an opportunity to read before he attached it near the top of my cage for the benefit and instruction of the audience: HORMAD FROM MORBUS, A MAN-LIKE MONSTER CAPTURED IN THE WILDS OF THE GREAT TOONOLIAN MARSHES.

I had been in my cage for about two hours when a detachment of the palace guard entered the avenue and chased all the spectators out of the zoo. A few minutes later there was a blare of trumpets at the far end of the avenue, and, looking, I saw a number of men and women approaching.

"What now?" I asked the red man in the cage next to me.

The fellow looked at me as though surprised that I had the power of speech. "Jal Had is coming to look at you," he said. "He is going to be very proud of you, because there is nothing else like you in the world."

"He may learn differently in time," I said, "and to his sorrow, for there are millions like me and their leaders are planning to overrun and conquer all Barsoom."

The red man laughed at that, but he would not have laughed if he had known what I knew.

The royal party was approaching, Jal Had walking a few paces ahead of the others. He was a gross-appearing man, with a cruel mouth and shifty eyes. He came and stopped before my cage; and as the others approached and stopped behind him, I saw that Janai was one of them. She looked up at me, and I saw tears forming in her eyes. "Splendid," said Jal Had, after he had examined me minutely for several moments. "I'll wager that there is not another specimen like this anywhere in the world." He turned toward his companions. "What do you think of it?" he demanded.

"It is wonderful," they all replied, practically in unison, that is, all but Janai. She remained silent.

Then Jal Had fixed his gaze upon Janai. "And what do you think of it, my love?" he asked.

"I thing a great deal of it," she replied. "Tor-dur-bar is my friend, and I think that it is a cruel shame to cage him up like this."

"You would like to have wild beasts roaming around the city, then?" he demanded.

"Tor-dur-bar is not a wild beast; he is a brave and loyal friend. But for him, I should have been long since dead; and though perhaps I had been better off, I shall never cease to appreciate the dangers and hardships that he endured for me."

"For that, he shall be rewarded, then," said Jal Had, magnanimously. "He shall receive the scraps from the royal table."

Now that was something. I, a noble of Helium, to be fed with the scraps from the table of Jal Had, Prince of Amhor. However, I consoled myself with the thought that scraps from his table would probably be far better fare than that ordinarily served to the beasts of the zoo, and I could easily swallow my pride along with his scraps.

Of course, I had no opportunity to converse with Janai, so I could not learn what had happened to her, nor what the future held for her, if she knew.

"Tell me something about yourself," demanded Jal Had. "Are you just a freak, or are there more like you? What were your father and mother like?"

"I had no father and mother," I replied, "and there are many more like me, millions of us."

"No father and mother?" he demanded. "But some sort of a creature must have laid the egg from which you hatched."

"I came from no egg," I replied.

"Well," said Jal Had, "you are not only the greatest freak I ever saw, but the greatest liar. Perhaps a good beating will teach you better manners than to lie to Jal Had."

"He has not lied," said Janai. "He has told you the truth."

"So you, too," he demanded of her, "you too, think I am a fool? I can have my women beaten, as well as my animals, if they do not behave themselves."

"You are proving definitely that you are a fool," I said, "for you have heard the truth from both of us, and yet do not believe it."

"Silence!" shouted an officer of the guard. "Shall I kill the presumptious beast, Jal Had?"

"No," replied the Prince. "He is too valuable. Perhaps later I shall have him beaten." I wondered who would have the temerity to enter my cage to beat me, I, who could tear an ordinary man limb from limb.

Jal Had turned and walked away, followed by the members of his party; and when they had left the avenue, the public was once more admitted; and, until dark, I had to endure the gaze and insults of a loud-mouthed rabble. Now I realized with what contempt caged beasts must look upon the human beings which gape and gawk at them.

After the crowds were expelled from the zoo, the animals were fed, for Jal Had had discovered that beasts in captivity thrive better if gaping crowds are not watching them at their food; and so his animals were allowed to feed in peace and in such solitude as their cages afforded. I was not fed with the others, but shortly afterward a slave boy came from Jal Had's palace with a hamper filled with the scraps from his table.

The boy was goggle-eyed with wonderment and awe as

he approached my cage and looked at me. There was a small door in the front of my cage near the floor through which the food could be passed to me; but the youth was evidently afraid to open it for fear that I might seize him.

"Do not be afraid," I said. "I shall not harm you. I am not a wild beast."

He came closer then and timidly opened the little door. "I am not afraid," he said; but I knew that he was.

"Where are you from?" I asked.

"From Duhor," he replied.

"A friend of a friend of mine lives there," I said.

"And who might that be?"

"Vad Varo," I replied.

"Ah, Vad Varo! I have seen him often. I was to have taken service in his guard when I finished my training. He married Valla Dia, our Princess. He is a great warrior. And who is your friend that is his friend?"

"John Carter, Prince of Helium, Warlord of Mars," I replied.

Then indeed did his eyes go wide. "John Carter, you know him? Who has not heard of him, the greatest swordsman of all Barsoom? But how could such as you be friend of John Carter?"

"It may seem strange to you," I admitted, "but the fact remains that John Carter is my best friend."

"But what do you know of John Carter?" demanded the red man in the adjoining cage. "I am from Helium; and there is no creature like you in the entire empire. I think you are a great liar. You lied to me, and you lied to Jal Had, and now you are lying to this young slave. What do you think you can gain by telling so many lies? Have you never heard that Martians pride themselves upon being truthful men?"

"I have not lied," I said.

"You do not even know what John Carter looks like," taunted the red man.

"He has black hair and grey eyes, and a lighter skin than yours," I replied; "and he came from Jasoom, and he is married to Dejah Thoris, Princess of Helium. When he came to Barsoom, he was captured by the green men of Thark. He has fought in Okar, the land of the yellow men in the far north; and he has fought therns in the Valley Dor; the length and breadth of Barsoom, he has fought; and when I saw him last, we were in Morbus together."

The red man looked surprised. "By my first ancestor," he

131

exclaimed, "but you do know a lot about John Carter. Perhaps you are telling the truth after all."

The young slave had looked at me with rapt attention. I could see that he was much impressed; and I hoped that I had won his confidence and that later I might win his friendship, for I wanted a friend in the palace of Jal Had, Prince of Amhor.

"So you have seen John Carter," he said. "You have talked with him, you have touched him. Ah, how wonderful!"

"Some day he may come to Amhor," I said, "and if he does, tell him that you knew Tor-dur-bar, and that you were kind to him; and John Carter will be your friend, too."

"I shall be as kind to you as I can," he said, "and if there is anything that I can do for you, I shall be glad to do it."

"There is something that you can do for me," I said.

"What is it?" he asked.

"Come closer, so that I may whisper it to you." He hesitated. "Do not be afraid; I shall not harm you."

Then he came close to the cage. "What is it?" he asked.

I kneeled and bent my lips close to his ear. "I wish to know all that you can learn about the girl, Janai; I mean, what is happening to her in the palace of Jal Had, and what is going to happen to her."

"I shall tell you all that I can learn," he said; and then he took his empty hamper and went away.

CHAPTER XXV

PRINCE IN A ZOO

MONOTONOUS DAYS CAME and went, relieved only by conversation with the red man in the adjoining cage, and by visits twice a day from the young slave from Duhor, whose name was Orm-O.

Quite a friendship developed between the red man from Helium and I. His name was Ur Raj; and when he told me it, I recalled having met him several years before. He was from Hastor, a city on the frontier of the empire, and had been a padwar aboard one of the warships stationed there. I asked him if he remembered an officer named Vor Daj, and he said he remembered him very well.

"Do you know him?" he inquired.

"Intimately," I replied. "In fact, there is nobody in the world whom I know so well."

"But how do you know him?" he demanded.

"He was at Morbus with John Carter," I replied.

"He was a splendid officer," he said. "I recall having a long conversation with him when the grand fleet came to Hastor."

"You and he discussed an invention that you were working upon that would detect and locate enemy ships at a great distance, identifying them by the sound of their motors. You had discovered that no two motors gave forth the same vibrations, and you had developed an instrument that recorded these vibrations accurately at great distances. You also introduced him to a very beautiful young lady whom you hoped to take as your mate."

Ur Raj's eyes went wide in astonishment. "But how in the world could you know of these matters?" he demanded. "You must have been very intimate with him indeed if he narrated to you the gist of conversations that took place years before with a comparative stranger."

"He told neither me nor any other about your invention," I replied, "because he promised you that he would not say anything about it until you had fully developed it and offered it to the navy of Helium."

"But then if he did not tell you, how could you know these things?" he demanded.

"That, you may never know," I replied; "but you may rest assured that Vor Daj never abused your confidence."

I believe that Ur Raj was a little in awe of me after that, believing that I had some supernatural or occult powers. I used to catch him gazing at me intently as he squatted upon the floor of his cage, doubtless trying to fathom what seemed an inexplicable mystery to him.

The slave boy, Orm-O, became quite friendly, telling me all that he could learn about Janai, which was little or nothing. I gathered from him that she was in no immediate danger, as Jal Had's oldest wife had taken her under her protection. Jal Had had several wives; and this first wife he feared above all things on earth. She had long objected to sharing the affections of Jal Had with other women; and she did not intend that the number should be increased, especially by the acquisition of so beautiful a young woman as Janai.

"It is rumored," said Orm-O, "that she will put Janai out of the way at the first opportunity. She is hesitating now only because of the fear that Jal Had, in his rage, would destroy her if she did so; but she may find a way to accomplish it without bringing suspicion upon herself. In fact, she has several times recently received Gantun Gur, the assassin of Amhor, who recently returned from captivity. I can tell you that I should not like to be Janai, especially if Gantun Gur listens too long to Vanuma and accepts a commission from her."

This information caused me considerable concern for the welfare of Janai. Of course, I felt quite certain that Gantun Gur would not kill her; but that would not keep Vanuma from finding some other means, if she had determined to destroy Janai. I asked Orm-O to warn Janai, and he said that he would if he ever had an opportunity.

The danger threatening Janai was constantly on my mind, and my inability to aid her drove me almost to distraction. If there were only something that I might do. But there was nothing. I seemed to be utterly helpless, and Janai's situation equally hopeless.

Sometimes we had dull days at the zoo; but as a rule there was a steady stream of people passing along the avenue between the cages, and almost always there was a little crowd gathered in front of my cage when the avenue was not jammed by those who came and stood looking at me for hours at a stretch. There were always new faces; but there were those that I had learned to recognize because they came so often; and then one day I saw Gantun Gur in the crowd. He shouldered his way toward me, eliciting much grumbling and some hard words; but when someone recognized him and his name was passed around, the spectators gave way before him, for no one wished to antagonize the assassin of Amhor. What a reputation the original must have gained!

"Kaor, Tor-dur-bar," he said, coming close to the cage.

"Kaor, Gantun Gur," I replied. "It is good to see you again; and I wish that I might speak to you privately."

"I will come back," he said, "after the visitors are expelled. You see, I am something of a privileged character in Amhor and around the palace. No one wishes to antagonize me, not even Jal Had."

I thought that the day would never end, that the visitors would never leave. The hours dragged interminably; but at last the guards drove the public out, and the carts containing food for the beasts were wheeled down the avenue. Then Orm-O came with his hamper of scraps; but there was no sign of Gantun Gur. I wondered if he had again deserted me, or if his boasted privilege was a myth. I was particularly anxious to see him, because I had finally evolved a plan which I thought might prove beneficial for Janai. I asked Orm-O for some word of her, but he only shook his head and said that he had not seen her around the palace for days.

"Perhaps Vanuma has had her destroyed," I suggested, fearfully.

"Perhaps," he said. "The last I heard was that she was not treating Janai so well as she had in the beginning. Some say that she whips her every night now."

I couldn't imagine Vanuma or anyone else whipping Janai, for she was not the type to take a whipping meekly.

It was almost dark and I had given up all hope of Gantun Gur, when I saw him approach my cage. "Kaor, Tor-dur-bar!" he said. "I was delayed; no less a person than Jal Had himself. He came to me in conversation."

"Whom does he wish killed now?" asked Ur Raj.

"He only wished to be certain that I was not planning on killing him," replied Gantun Gur. "Do you know that I would rather be what I am, head of the Assassins' Guild, than to be Prince of Amhor! My power is unlimited; everyone fears me, for, while I am known, all my assassins are not; and even those who might plot against me fear to do so lest my spies learn of it."

"You have come a long way from the Laboratory Building, Gantun Gur," I said, with a smile. "But tell me, does Janai still live? Is she well? Is she safe?"

"She lives and is well, but she is not safe; she never can be safe in Amhor. At least her life will never be safe as long as Vanuma lives. Of course, I do not need to tell you that neither I nor any of my assassins will destroy Janai; but Vanuma may find someone else to do it, or even do it herself in desperation; so I have come to the conclusion that the best thing that I can do is to have Vanuma assassinated."

"No, no," I objected. "The moment Vanuma were out of the way, there would be none to protect Janai from Jal Had."

"That is right," said Gantun Gur, scratching his head. "I had not taken that phase of the matter into consideration. As a matter of fact, it would not be so bad for Janai, for then she would become Princess of Amhor; and from what I have seen of Jal Had's other wife, Janai would rule undisputed queen."

"But she does not wish to marry Jal Had," I said. "Vor Daj loves her. We must save her for him."

"Vor Daj," said Gantun Gur, "lying as one dead in the pits

135

beneath the Laboratory Building of Morbus, certainly surrounded and perhaps long since devoured by the horror that spreads from Vat Room No. 4. No, no, Tor-dur-bar, while I admire your loyalty to Vor Daj, I think that it is wasted. Neither you, nor I, nor Janai will ever see him again."

"Nevertheless, we must do what we can to save Janai for him; for I, for one, have not given up hope that Vor Daj some day will be rescued."

"Well, have you a plan, then?" he asked.

"Yes," I said, "I have."

"What is it?" he demanded.

"Get word to Vanuma, even if you have to tell her yourself, that Jal Had has learned that she is attempting to hire assassins to destroy Janai, and that he has sworn that if Janai dies, no matter what the cause, he will immediately destroy Vanuma."

"Not a bad idea," said Gantun Gur. "I can get that word to her immediately through one of her female slaves."

"I shall breathe more easily when I know that you have done it," I said.

I certainly slept better that night than I had for a long time, because I felt that, temporarily at least, Janai was safe. It was well for my peace of mind that I did not know what the next morning was to bring.

CHAPTER XXVI

THE BITE OF THE ADDER

MY CELL WAS divided laterally by a partition, the front of the cell being open on the avenue, the rear consisting of a dark compartment in which there was a single, small window and a heavy door in the back wall. This was my bedroom, and my bed was a pile of the moss-like, ochre vegetation that covers the dead sea bottoms of Barsoom. A sliding door, that was raised and lowered by means of a rope passing over a pulley and thence outside the back of the cage, connected the two compartments. When I was in the front compartment, attendants could lower the door and enter the rear compartment for the purpose of cleaning it out, and vice versa, no one venturing to come into either compartment alone with me. I must say for Jal Had, that he had our cages kept reasonably clean; but that was because he realized that he could thus keep us in a more healthy condition and not because of any humanitarian instincts which he possessed.

The morning after Gantun Gur's visit, I was awakened by the beating of drums and the mournful notes of wind instruments producing music that sounded very much like a dirge. Further sleep was impossible; so I crawled out into the daylight of my front compartment where I saw Ur Raj standing with his face pressed against the bars of his cage, looking toward the palace.

"Why the music?" I asked. "Are they celebrating something?"

"Perhaps they are at that," he replied, with a smile, "though that music means that a member of the royal family is dead."

"Let us hope that it is Jal Had," I said.

"Probably no such luck," returned Ur Raj.

The attendants were coming along the avenue, feeding the animals; and when they reached Ur Raj's cage we asked them who was dead; but they told us that it was none of our business, and passed on. Of course, there was no reason why they should not have told us, if they had known; but it seemed to give them a feeling of greater importance if they treated us like wild beasts rather than like men, and wild beasts are not supposed to know anything of the affairs of their masters.

The green man in the adjoining cage had never been a very friendly neighbor. I think he resented the fact that I attracted more attention than he. He never addressed me, and had answered in monosyllables or not at all, the few times that I had spoken to him; but, of course, that might have been because they are naturally a sullen and taciturn race; but now, quite unexpectedly, he spoke to me.

"If Jal Had is dead," he said, "there will be confusion for several days. I have been here a long time, and I have learned much. I have learned that there are several who would like to succeed Jal Had, and if he is dead Amhor may have a civil war on her hands. Then would be a good time for us to try to escape."

"If I had thought that there was any chance of escaping," I said, "I would not have waited for Jal Had to die."

"Until something happens that disrupts the discipline of the guards and throws the city into turmoil," said the green man, "no plan of escape would have a chance of success, but when that happens I have a plan that may succeed."

"What is it?" I asked.

"Come closer to the bars, and I will whisper it to you. I do not wish any to overhear. One man could not accomplish the thing alone, but I believe that I can trust you and the red man next to you. I have watched you both carefully, and I believe that you have the courage and the intelligence to help me carry the plan to a successful conclusion." Then, in a whisper, he explained to me in detail the idea that he had in mind. It was not bad, and perhaps had some element of success. The green man asked me to explain to Ur Raj, and I did so. The red man listened intently and then nodded his head.

"Whether it should fail or succeed," he said, "it is at least better than remaining here in captivity for life."

"I quite agree with you," I said, "and if only my life were at stake, I should be willing to make the attempt at any time; but I must await some opportunity to rescue Janai with me."

"But what can be your interest in the red girl, Janai?" demanded Ur Raj. "She certainly wouldn't give a second glance at anyone as hideous as you."

"I promised Vor Daj that I would protect her," I said; "and so I cannot go without her."

"I see," said Ur Raj; "so inasmuch as no plan of escape will succeed, we might as well plan on taking Janai with us. It won't complicate matters in the least. Fortunately, they cannot keep us from dreaming dreams, Tor-dur-bar; and as that is about all the happiness that we have a right to expect, we might as well make the most of it and dream really worthwhile dreams. I shall dream that we shall be successful; that we destroy Jal Had, and that I become Prince of Amhor. I shall make you one of my dwars, Tor-dur-bar. In fact, I appoint you now." He laughed heartily at his little joke, and I joined in with him.

"But I was an odwar in Morbus," I said.

"Oh, very well, you shall be an odwar here, then. Consider yourself promoted."

The green man saw nothing funny in what we were saying, taking it all literally. They have no sense of humor as we understand it, and never smile or laugh except when witnessing the sufferings of others. I have seen them fairly roll on the ground with laughter while watching the agony of some victim upon which they were reeking the most fiendish tortures. Further conversation between us on this subject was interrupted by the arrival of Orm-O with his hamper of scraps for my breakfast.

"What has happened, Orm-O?" I asked him. "Why the music?"

"Do you mean that you have not heard?" he asked. "Vanuma is dead. One of her slaves told me that there was no doubt but that she had been poisoned; and Jal Had is suspected."

Vanuma dead! What would become of Janai now?

We inmates of the zoo were little affected by what went on in the palace following the death of Vanuma, but for a single circumstance. Until after the funeral, which occurred five days later, the palace grounds were closed to the public, and so we looked forward to a period of what I felt would be a most delightful interlude of peace and quiet; but I soon discovered that it was not as enjoyable as I had anticipated, for I found the monotony of it almost unendurable. Strange as it may seem, I missed the gaping rabble and learned that they afforded us quite as much amusement, entertainment, and distraction as we offered them.

During this time, I learned something from Orm-O which set my mind at rest insofar as Janai was concerned for at least a period of time. He told me that court etiquette required a period of mourning of twenty-seven days, during which the royal family eschewed all pleasures; but he had also told me that immediately following this period Jal Had planned to take Janai in marriage.

Another thing that I learned from him was that the family of Vanuma believed that Jal Had had caused Vanuma to be poisoned. They were powerful nobles of royal descent, and among them was one who aspired to be Prince of Amhor. This Dur Ajmad was far more popular than Jal Had, his influence with the army, outside of Jal Had's personal troops, being great.

Had it not been for Orm-O, we in the zoo would have known nothing of all this; but he kept us well informed, so that we were able to follow the happenings in the palace and the city quite as well as any of the ordinary citizens of Amhor. As the days passed, I could see that the temper of the people who visited the zoo had changed. They were tense and nervous, and many were the glances cast in the direction of the palace. More people than ever jammed the avenue between the cages, but I felt that they were there more to see what might happen in the palace grounds than to look at us. Whispering groups gathered, paying no attention to us; and they were evidently concerned with more important things than wild beasts.

Then one day near the close of the mourning period, I heard, early in the morning, the humming staccato of Martian firearms; and there were trumpet calls and shouted orders. Guards closed the gates that had just been opened to admit the public; and with the exception of the detail that remained to guard the gate, attendants and warriors alike ran in the direction of the palace.

It was all very exciting; but in the excitement I did not forget what it might mean to me and Janai, nor did I forget the plan that the green man and Ur Raj and I had discussed; and so, when one of the last of the attendants came running down the avenue toward the palace, I threw myself upon the floor of my cage and writhed in apparent agony, as I screamed to him to come to me. I didn't know whether or not the ruse would work, for the man must have wanted to go with the others and see what was happening at the palace; but I banked on the fact that he must realize that if anything happened to one of his charges and especially so valuable a one as I, Jal Had would unquestionably punish him for deserting his post; and Jal Had's punishments were quite often fatal.

The fellow hesitated a moment as he turned and looked in my direction. He started on again toward the palace but after a few steps he turned and ran to my cage. "What is the matter with you, beast?" he cried.

"There is a strange reptile in my sleeping den," I cried. "It has bitten me, and I am going to die."

"Where did it bite you?" he demanded.

"On the hand," I cried. "Come look."

He came close, and when he did so I reached between the bars quickly and seized him by the throat. So quickly and so tightly did I close upon his windpipe that he had no opportunity to make an outcry. Ur Raj and the green man were pressed against the bars of their cages watching me. Only we three saw the guard die.

I dragged the body upward until I could seize the keys that hung upon a ring by his harness. Then I let it drop to the ground. I easily reached the padlock that secured the door in the front of the cage, and in a few seconds I was out on the ground. From there I crawled quickly beneath the cages to the rear where my activities would be hidden from view from any who might pass along the avenue. I released the green man and Ur Raj, and for a moment we stood there discussing the advisability of carrying out in full the plan we had contemplated. It offered considerable risk for us, but we felt that it might create such a diversion that in the

140

ensuing confusion we might have a better chance of escaping.

"Yes," agreed Ur Raj, "the more confusion there is, the better chance we shall have to reach the palace and find your Janai."

I must say that the whole plan was hare-brained and hopeless. It had perhaps one chance in a hundred million of succeeding.

"Very well," I said, "come on."

Back of the cages we found a number of the staves and goads used by the attendants to control the beasts, and armed with these we started toward the lower cages nearest the gate and farthest from the palace. I was also armed with the shortsword and dagger I had taken from the attendant I had killed, but I could not hope that they would be of much use to me in the event that our plans miscarried.

Beginning at the cage nearest the gate, we released the animals, driving them ahead of us along the rear of the cages in the direction of the palace.

I had been fearful that we would be unable to control them and that they would turn upon us and destroy us; but I soon learned that from experience they had become afraid of the sharp goads used by the keepers, with which we threatened and prodded them along. Even the two great apts and the white apes moved sullenly before us. At first there was little noise or confusion, only low growls from the carnivores and the nervous snorting of the herbivorous animals; but as we proceeded and the number and variety of the beasts increased, so did the volume of sounds until the air rang with the bellowing of the zitidars and the squeals of the maddened throats, and the roars and growls of banths and apts and the scores of other beasts moving nervously ahead of us.

A gate that is always kept closed separates the zoo from the grounds immediately surrounding the palace. This, the attendants in their excitement had left open today, and through it we drove the beasts into the palace grounds without interference.

By now every beast in the horrible pack, excited to a high pitch of nervous tension by this unaccustomed liberty and the voices of their fellows, had joined in the horrid diapason of ferocity so that no one within the palace grounds or, for that matter, for some distance beyond them, could have failed to hear, and now I saw the attendants who had deserted their posts running to meet us. The beasts saw them, too, and some of the more intelligent, such as the great

141

white apes, must have remembered indignities and cruelties heaped upon them during their captivity, for with snarls and growls and roars of rage they sprang forward to meet the keepers, and fell upon them and destroyed them; and then, further incited by this taste of blood and revenge, they moved on toward the soldiers defending the gates, which were being threatened by the troops of Dur Ajmad.

This was precisely what we had hoped for, as it created a diversion which permitted Ur Raj, the green man, and me to enter a side door of the palace unobserved.

At last I had succeeded in entering the palace where Janai was a prisoner; but a plan for turning the situation to our advantage was still as remote as the farther moon. I was in the palace, but where in that great pile was Janai?

CHAPTER XXVII

FLIGHT INTO JEOPARDY

THE ROOMS AND corridors of that portion of the palace which we had entered were deserted, the inmates being either in hiding or defending the gates.

"And now that we are here," demanded Bal Tab, the green man, "what do we do next? Where is the red woman?"

"It is a large palace to search," said Ur Raj. "Even if we meet with no interference, it would take a long time; but certainly before long we shall find warriors barring our way."

"Someone is coming down this corridor," said Bal Tab. "I can hear him."

The corridor curved to the left just ahead of us, and presently around this curve came a youth whom I recognized instantly. It was Orm-O. He ran quickly toward me.

"From one of the upper windows, I saw you enter the palace," he said, "and I hurried to meet you as quickly as I could."

"Where is Janai?" I demanded.

"I will show you," he said; "but if I am found out, I shall be killed. Perhaps you are too late, for Jal Had has gone to visit her in her apartments, even though the period of mourning is not over."

"Hurry," I snapped, and Orm-O set off at a trot along the corridor, followed by Ur Raj, Bal Tab, and me. He led us to the bottom of a spiral ramp and told us to ascend to the third level where we should turn to the right and follow a corridor to its end. There we should find the door leading into Janai's apartments.

"If Jal Had is with Janai, the corridor will be guarded," he said, "and you will have to fight, but you will not have to contend with firearms as Jal Had, fearing assassination, permits no one but himself to carry firearms in the palace."

After thanking Orm-O, the three of us ascended the spiral ramp, and as we reached the third level I saw two warriors standing before a door at the end of a short corridor. Behind that door would be Jal Had and Janai.

The warriors saw us as soon as we saw them, and they came toward us with drawn swords.

"What do you want here?" demanded one of them.

"I wish to see Jal Had," I replied.

"You cannot see Jal Had," he said. "Go back to your cages where you belong."

For answer, Bal Tab felled the warrior with a blow from the metal shod goad that he carried, and almost simultaneously I engaged the other in a duel with swords. The fellow was a remarkably good swordsman, but he could not cope with one who had been a pupil of John Carter and who had the added advantage of an abnormally long reach and great strength.

I finished him quickly as I did not wish to delay much, nor did I wish to add to his sufferings.

Bal Tab was smiling, for it amused him to see men die. "You have a fine sword arm," he said, which was high praise from a green Martian.

Stepping over the body of my antagonist, I threw open the door and entered the room beyond, a small ante-room which was vacant. At the far end of this room was another door, beyond which I could hear the sound of voices raised in anger or excitement. Crossing quickly, I entered the second room where I found Jal Had holding Janai in his arms. She was struggling to escape, and striking at him. His face was red with anger, and I saw him raise his fist to strike her.

"Stop!" I cried, and then they both turned and saw me.

"Tor-dur-bar!" cried Janai, and there was a note of relief in her tone.

When Jal Had saw us he pushed Janai roughly from him and whipped out his radium pistol. I leaped for him, but before I could reach him, a metal shod goad whizzed by my shoulder and passed through the heart of the Prince of Amhor before he could level his pistol or squeeze the trigger.

143

Bal Tab it was who had cast the goad, and to him I probably owed my life.

I think we were all a little surprised and shaken by the suddenness and enormity of the thing that had taken place, and for a moment we stood there in silence looking down at the body of Jal Had.

"Well," said Ur Raj, presently, "he is dead; and now what are we going to do?"

"The palace and the palace grounds are filled with his retainers," said Janai. "If they discover what we have done, we shall all be killed."

"We three should give them a battle they would long remember," said Bal Tab.

"If there were some place where we might hide until after dark," said Ur Raj, "I am sure that we can get out of the palace grounds, and we might even be able to leave the city."

"Do you know any place where we might hide until after dark?" I asked Janai.

"No," she said, "I know of no place where they would not search."

"What is on the level above us?" I asked.

"The royal hangar," she replied, "where Jal Had's private airships are kept."

Involuntarily I voiced an exclamation of relief. "What luck!" I exclaimed. "Nothing could suit our purpose better than one of Jal Had's fliers."

"But the hangars are well guarded," said Janai. "I have often seen the warriers marching past my door to relieve the hangar guards. There were never less than ten of them."

"There may not be so many today," said Ur Raj, "as Jal Had needed all his force to defend the palace gates."

"If there were twenty," said Bal Tab, "it would make a better fight. Let us hope that there are not too few."

I gave Jal Had's radium pistol to Ur Raj, and then the four of us went out into the corridor and ascended the ramp that led to the hangar on the roof. I sent Ur Raj ahead because he was smaller than either Bal Tab or I, and could reconnoiter with less likelihood of being discovered; also, the fact that he was a red man made it advantageous to use him thus, as he would less quickly arouse suspicion than either Bal Tab or myself. We three trailed a short distance behind him, and when he reached a point where he could get a view of the roof we halted and waited.

Presently he returned to us. "There are but two men on guard," he said. "It will be easy."

"We'll rush them," I suggested. "If we take them by surprise, it may not be necessary to kill them." Although an experienced man who has participated in many conflicts, I still dislike seeing men die and especially by my own hands, if matters can be arranged otherwise; but the chaps who guarded the royal hangar on the roof did not seem to care whether they lived or died for they charged us the moment they saw us; and though I promised not to harm them if they surrendered, they kept on coming until there was nothing for us to do but engage them.

Just before they reached us, one of them spoke quietly to the other, who turned and ran as fast as he could across the roof. Then his valiant companion engaged us; but I caught a glimpse of the second man disappearing through a trap in the roof. Evidently he had gone to summon aid while his fellow sacrificed his life to detain us. The instant that I realized this, I leaped in to close quarters and dispatched the warrior, though I must say that I never before killed a man with less relish. This simple warrior was a hero, if ever there was one; and it seemed a shame to take his life, but it was his or ours.

Knowing that pursuit might develop immediately, I summoned the others to follow me and hastened into the hangar where I quickly selected what appeared to be a reasonably fast flier which would accommodate all of us.

I knew that Ur Raj could pilot a ship; and so I ordered him to the controls, and a moment later we were gliding smoothly out of the hangar and across the roof. As we took off, I looked down into the palace grounds from which rose the cries of the beasts and the shouts of the warriors; and even as I looked I saw the gate fall and the men of Dur Ajmad swarm through to overwhelm the remnants of Jal Had's forces.

As we rose in the air, I saw a patrol boat some distance away turn and head for us. I immediately ordered Bal Tab and Janai below, and after giving some instructions to Ur Raj I followed them so that none of us might be seen by members of the crew of the patrol boat.

The latter approached us rapidly, and when it was in speaking distance asked us who we had aboard and where we were headed. Following my instructions, Ur Raj replied that Jal Had was below and that he had given orders not to divulge our destination. The commander of the patrol boat may have had his doubts as to the veracity of the statement, but evidently he felt that he did not care to take a chance of antagonizing his prince in the event that he were aboard and had given such instructions; so he fell off and let us continue on our way; but presently he started trailing us, and before we had passed beyond the limits of the city I saw at least a dozen fliers in pursuit. The hangar guard who had escaped had evidently raised the alarm. Perhaps, even, they had found the body of Jal Had. In any event, it was quite evident that we were being pursued; and when the other ships overtook the patrol and spoke, it too came after us at full speed.

CHAPTER XXVIII

THE GREAT FLEET

THE FLIER WE had commandeered was of about the same speed as the larger vessels that were pursuing us; but the patrol boat was faster, and it was evident that she would eventually overhaul us.

A hasty survey of the boat revealed that there were rifles in their racks below deck and a small gun at bow and astern above. They all fired the ordinary Martian exploding projectiles which have been standard for ages. A single, direct hit in any vital part of the ship might easily disable it, and I knew that as soon as the patrol plane came within range it would commence firing. I had come on deck as soon as I had realized that we were no longer deceiving the Amhorians, and I was standing beside Ur Raj urging him to greater speed.

"She is doing her limit now," he said; "but they are still gaining on us. However, I don't think we need to worry greatly. You may not have noticed it, but the hull of this ship is well protected, probably better armored than the other ships because it was used by Jal Had, personally. Only by scoring a direct hit on the controls or the rudder, can they put us out of commission, unless they are able to get very close and give us a broadside; but with our guns we ought to be able to prevent that."

Janai and Bal Tab had joined me on deck, and we three stood watching the pursuing patrol boat, which was gaining on us steadily.

"There!" said Janai. "They have opened fire."

"It fell short and would have been wide anyway," said Bal Tab.

"But they will soon correct that and get our range," I prophesied.

I told Janai and Bal Tab to go below as there was no sense in risking their lives on deck unnecessarily.

"When we are in rifle range, Bal Tab," I told him, "I shall send for you; and you may bring up two or three rifles from below."

I then went to the stern gun and trained it on the oncoming patrol boat as another shot fell just short of us. Then I trained our gun very carefully and fired.

"Fine!" cried Janai. "You scored a hit the first time." I turned to see both her and Bal Tab kneeling behind me. We were screened by the gun shield, but I still thought it too dangerous; but she would not go below nor either would Bal Tab except only to bring up several rifles and a larger supply of ammunition.

My shot, while a direct hit, had evidently done little or no harm for it neither slowed up the craft nor interfered with its firing.

Presently the patrol boat commenced to veer off slightly to the right with the possible intention of getting into a position from which it could pour broadsides into us.

We were both firing continuously now, and every now and then a shell would strike against the gunshield or the hull and explode.

I cautioned Ur Raj to keep on a straight course, since, if we tried to keep our stern and smallest target always presented to the pursuing enemy, we should have to alter our course and would be driven into a wide curve that would permit the larger vessels to overhaul us. Then we should most certainly be destroyed or captured.

This running fight continued until Amhor lay far behind. We were speeding above vast stretches where once Mars' mighty oceans rolled, now barren waste where only the wild, nomadic green men roved. The patrol boat had steadily gained on us, and the fleet of larger vessels had crept up a little, showing that they were a trifle faster than our flier. The patrol boat was slowly creeping up opposite us but still at a considerable distance. They had ceased firing, and now they signalled us to surrender; but for reply Bal Tab and I turned both the bow and stern guns upon them. They returned our fire, giving us a broadside with all their guns. I dragged Janai down beside me behind the gunshield; but Bal Tab

147

had not been so fortunate. I saw him straighten to his full height and topple backward over the side of the flier.

I regretted the loss of Bal Tab, not only because it reduced our defensive force but because of the loss of a loyal comrade and a fine fighting man. However, he was gone, and mourning would do no good. He had died as he would have wished to die, fighting; and his body lay where he would have wished it to lie, on the ochre moss of a dead sea bottom.

Projectiles were now exploding continually against the armored sides of our craft and the gunshield which was our protection. Ur Raj had ample protection in the pilot's compartment, which was heavily armored.

We three seemed safe enough if we kept behind our protection; but how long the armored side of the flier could withstand this constant bombardment of exploding shells, I did not know.

Attracting Ur Raj's attention, I signalled him to rise and endeavor to get above the patrol boat, for if we could fire down upon her from above, we might disable her.

As we started to rise, Ur Raj called to me and pointed ahead. A sight met my eyes that fairly took my breath away. Approaching, far aloft and already almost above us, was a fleet of great battleships that we had not observed because of our preoccupation with the fight in which we had been engaged.

I was certain from the size and number of them that they were not ships of Amhor; but from our position below them I could not read the insignias upon their bows nor see the colors flying from their superstructures. However, no matter what nation they represented, we would be no worse off in their hands than in the hands of the Amhorians; so I instructed Ur Raj to continue to set his course for them and to try to get between them and the patrol boat, hoping that the latter would hold its fire rather than take a chance of hitting one of the great ships of the fleet whose big guns could have destroyed it in an instant; nor was I wrong in my conjecture, for the patrol boat ceased firing though it continued to pursue us.

We were now rapidly approaching the leading ship of the fleet. I could see men peering over the sides at us, and presently the great craft slowed down.

As we arose closer to its bow, Ur Raj suddenly cried out in exaltation, "A fleet from Helium!" And then I, too, saw the insignia on the ship's bow, and my heart leaped for I knew that Janai was saved.

148

Now they hailed us, demanding to know who we were. "Ur Raj of Hastor," I replied, "a padwar in the Navy of Helium, and two of his friends escaping from imprisonment in the City of Amhor."

They ordered us to come aboard, then, and Ur Raj piloted the craft across their rail and set it down on the broad deck of the battleship.

Officers and men looked at me in astonishment as I dropped to the deck and lifted Janai down. Then Ur Raj joined us.

In the meantime, the Amhorian patrol boat had evidently discovered the identity of their fleet, for it turned about and was speeding back toward its sister ships; and soon all those that had been pursuing us were headed back toward Amhor at full speed; for they knew that Ur Raj was from Helium, and they feared reprisals for having held him in captivity.

Janai, Ur Raj, and I were taken before the commanding officer where Ur Raj had no difficulty in convincing them of his identity. "And these other two?" demanded the officer, indicating Janai and me.

"I am a friend of Vor Daj," I replied, "and so is this girl, Janai. I have served John Carter, too, faithfully. He will be glad to know that I am alive and well."

"You are Tor-dur-bar?" asked the officer.

"Yes," I replied, "but how could you know that?"

"This fleet was on its way to Amhor in search of you and the girl, Janai."

"But how in the world could you have known that we were at Amhor?" I asked, amazed.

"It is quite simple," he replied. "The fleet was bringing John Carter and Ras Thavas back to Morbus. Yesterday we were sailing low over the Great Toonolian Marshes when we saw a red man being pursued by savages. Their canoes were about to overtake his when we dropped a bomb among them, dispersing them. Then we dropped lower, and with landing tackle brought the man aboard. He said that his name was Pandar, and that he was escaping from Morbus; and when John Carter questioned him he learned that a flier from Amhor had captured you and the girl, Janai. The fleet was immediately ordered to Amhor to effect your rescue."

"And you arrived none too soon," I said; "but tell me, John Carter and Ras Thavas both live?"

"Yes," he said; "they are aboard the Ruzaar."

I have always prided myself that I have perfect control over my emotions; but with this final proof that John Carter

149

and Ras Thavas both lived, I came as close to breaking down as I ever had in my life. The relief from long months of doubt and uncertainty almost proved my undoing; but I held myself together, and then in a moment another doubt raised its ugly head. John Carter and Ras Thavas lived; but was the body of Vor Daj still in existence? And, if so, was it within the power of man to recover it?

CHAPTER XXIX

BACK TOWARD MORBUS

WE WERE SOON transferred to the Ruzaar, where I received a warm greeting from John Carter and Ras Thavas.

When I told my story, and Ur Raj had assured them that there were no more Heliumetic prisoners in Amhor, John Carter ordered the fleet about; and it headed again toward Morbus.

Ras Thavas was much concerned when I told him about the accident that had occurred in Vat Room No. 4 and its results.

"That is bad," he said, "very bad. We may never be able to stop it. Let us hope that it has not reached the body of Vor Daj."

"Oh, don't suggest such a thing," cried Janai. "Vor Daj must be saved."

"It was to rescue Vor Daj that I returned with this fleet," said John Carter, "and you may rest assured that it will not return without him, unless he has been destroyed."

In fear and trembling, I inquired of John Carter the state of Dejah Thoris's health.

"Thanks to Ras Thavas, she has completely recovered," he replied. "Every great surgeon of Helium had given her up; but Ras Thavas, the miracle worker, restored her to perfect health."

"Did you have any difficulty in returning to Helium from Morbus?" I asked.

"We had little else," he replied. "From Morbus to Phundahl was almost one continuous battle with insects, beasts, reptiles, and savage men. How we survived it and won through is a mystery to me; but Dur-dan and Ras Thavas gave a good account of themselves with sword and dagger, and we came through almost to the flier without the loss of one of our number. Then, just the day before we reached it, Dur-dan was killed in a battle with some wild savages—the last we were to encounter in the Marshes. The journey between Morbus and Phundahl took up most of the time; but then, of course, we had to spend some time in Helium while Dejah Thoris was undergoing treatment. I felt convinced that you would pull through some way. You were powerful, intelligent, and resourceful; but I am afraid that my confidence would have been undermined had I known of what had happened in Vat Room No. 4."

"It is a terrible catastrophe," I said, "perhaps a world catastrophe, and as horrifying a sight as any that you have ever witnessed. There is no combatting it, for even if you cut it to pieces it continues to grow and to spread."

That evening as I was walking on deck, I saw Janai standing alone at the rail. Knowing how repulsive I must be to her I never forced my company upon her; but this time she stopped me.

"Tor-dur-bar," she said, "I wonder if I have ever adequately thanked you for all that you have done for me?"

"I want no thanks," I said. "It is enough that I have been able to serve you and Vor Daj."

She looked at me very closely. "What will it mean to you, Tor-dur-bar, if Vor Daj's body is never recovered?"

"I shall have lost a friend," I said.

"And you will come to Helium to live?"

"I do not know that I shall care to live," I said.

"Why?" she demanded.

"Because there is no place in the world for such a hideous monster as I."

"Do not say that, Tor-dur-bar," she said, kindly. "You are not hideous, because you have a good heart. At first, before I knew you, I thought that you were hideous; but now, my friend, I see only the beauty and nobility of your character."

That was very sweet of her, and I told her so; but it didn't alter the fact that I was so hideous that I knew I should constantly be frightening women and children should I consent to go to Helium.

"Well, I think your appearance will make little difference in Helium," she said, "for I am convinced that you will have many friends; but what is to become of me if Vor Daj is not rescued?"

"You need have no fear. John Carter will see to that."

"But John Carter is under no obligation to me," she insisted.

"Nevertheless, he will take care of you."

"And you will come to see me, Tor-dur-bar?" she asked.

"If you wish me to," I said; but I knew that Tor-dur-bar would never live to go to Helium.

She looked at me in silence and steadily for a moment, and then she said, "I know what is in your mind, Tor-dur-bar. You will never come to Helium as you are; but now that Ras Thavas has returned, why can he not give your brain a new body, as he did for so many other less worthy hormads?"

"Perhaps," I replied; "but where shall I find a body?"

"There is Vor Daj's," she said, in a whisper.

"You mean," I said, "that you would like my brain in the body of Vor Daj?"

"Why not?" she asked. "It is your brain that has been my best and most loyal friend. Sytor told me that Vor Daj's brain had been destroyed. Perhaps it has. If that is true, I know that he lied when he said that you caused it to be destroyed; for I know you better now and know that you would not have so wronged a friend; but if by chance it has been destroyed, what could be better for me than that the brain of my friend animate the body of one whom I so admired?"

"But wouldn't you always say to yourself, 'this body has the brain of a hormad? It is not Vor Daj; it is just a thing that grew in a Vat.' "

"No," she replied. "I do not think that it would make any difference. I do not think that it would be difficult for me to convince myself that the brain and the body belonged together, just as, on the contrary, it has been difficult to conceive that the brain which animates the body of Tor-dur-bar orginated in a vat of slimy, animal tissue."

"If Ras Thavas should find me a handsome body," I said, jokingly, "then Vor Daj would have a rival, I can assure you."

She shot me a quizzical look. "I do not think so," she said.

I wondered just what she meant by that and why she looked at me so peculiarly. It was not likely that she had guessed the truth, since it was inconceivable that any man would have permitted his brain to be transferred to the body of a hormad. Could she have meant that Vor Daj could have no successful rival?

It was night when we approached the Great Toonolian

Marshes. The great fleet sailed majestically over the City of Phundahl; the lighted city gleamed through the darkness below us, but no patrol boat ventured aloft to question us. Our ships were all lighted and must have been visible for a long time before we passed over the city; but Phundahl, weak in ships, would challenge no strange fleet the size of ours. I could well imagine that the Jed of Phundahl breathed more easily as we vanished into the eastern night.

CHAPTER XXX

THE END OF TWO WORLDS

THE DESOLATE WASTES of the Great Toonolian Marshes over which we passed that night took on a strange, weird beauty and added mystery in the darkness. Their waters reflected the myriad stars which the thin air of Mars reveals; and the passing moons were reflected back from the still lagoons or touched the rocky islets with a soft radiance that transformed them into isles of enchantment. Occasionally, we saw the campfires of savages, and faintly to our ears rose the chanting of barbaric songs and the booming of drums muffled by distance; all punctuated by the scream or bellow of some savage thing.

"The last of the great oceans," said John Carter, who had joined me at the rail. "Its eventual passing will doubtless mark the passing of a world, and Mars will hurtle on through all eternity peopled by not even a memory of its past grandeur."

"It saddens me to think of it," I said.

"And me, too," he replied.

"But you could return to Earth," I reminded him.

He smiled. "I do not think that either of us need worry about the end of Mars; at least, not for another million years, perhaps."

I laughed. "Somehow, when you spoke of it, it seemed as though the end were very near," I said.

"Comparatively speaking, it is," he replied. "Here we have only a shallow marshland to remind us of the mighty oceans which once rolled across the major portion of Barsoom. On Earth, the waters cover three quarters of the globe, reaching a depth of over five miles; yet, eventually the same fate will overtake that planet. The mountains will wash

153

down into the seas; the seas will evaporate; and some day all that will be left to mark their great oceans will be another Toonolian Marsh in some barren waste where the great Pacific Ocean rolls today."

"You make me sad," I said.

"Well, let's not worry about it, then," he laughed. "We have much more important matters to consider than the end of the two worlds. The fate of a friend transcends that of a planet. What shall you do if your body cannot be recovered?"

"I shall never return to Helium with this body," I replied.

"I cannot blame you. We shall have to find you another body."

"No," I said. "I have given the matter a great deal of thought, and I have come to a final decision. If my own body has been destroyed, I shall destroy this body, too, and the brain with it. There are far more desirable bodies than mine, of course; and yet I am so attached to it that I should not care to live in the body of another."

"Do not decide too hastily, Vor Daj."

"Tor-dur-bar, my Prince," I corrected.

"Why carry on the masquerade longer?" he demanded.

"Because she does not know," I said.

He nodded. "You think it might make a difference with her?" he asked.

"I am afraid that she could never forget this inhuman face and body, and that she might always wonder if the brain, too, were not the brain of a hormad, even though it reposed in the skull of Vor Daj. No one knows but you and Ras Thavas and I, my prince. I beg of you that you will never divulge the truth to Janai."

"As you wish," he said; "though I am quite sure that you are making a mistake. If she cares for you, it will make no difference to her; if she does not care for you, it will make no difference to you."

"No," I said. "I want to forget Tor-dur-bar, myself, and I certainly want her to forget him."

"That she will never do," he said, "for, from what she has told me, she entertains a very strong affection for Tor-dur-bar. He is Vor Daj's most dangerous rival."

"Don't," I begged. "The very idea is repulsive."

"It is the character that makes the man," said John Carter, "not the clay which is its abode."

"No, my friend," I replied, "no amount of philosophizing

154

could make Tor-dur-bar a suitable mate for any red woman, least of all, Janai."

"Perhaps you are right," he agreed; "but after the great sacrifice that you have made for her, I feel that you deserve a better reward than death by your own hand."

"Well," I replied, "tomorrow will probably decide the matter for us; and already I see the first streak of dawn above the horizon."

He thought in silence for a few moments, and then he said, "Perhaps the least of the difficulties which may confront us will be reaching 3-17 and the body of Vor Daj. What concerns me more than that is the likelihood that the entire Laboratory Building may be filled with the mass from Vat Room No. 4, in which event it will be practically impossible to reach Ras Thavas's laboratory which contains the necessary paraphernalia for the delicate operation of returning your brain to your own body."

"I anticipated that," I replied; "and on my way out of Morbus, I took everything that was necessary to 3-17."

"Good!" he exclaimed. "My mind is greatly relieved. Ras Thavas and I have both been deeply concerned by what amounted to his practical certainty that we should never be able to reach his laboratory. He believes that it is going to be necessary to destroy Morbus before we can check the growth from Vat No. 4."

It was daylight when we approached Morbus. The ships, with the exception of the Ruzaar, which carried us, were dispatched to circle the island to discover how far the mass from Vat Room No. 4 had spread.

The Ruzaar, dropping to within a few yards of the ground, approached the little island where lay the tunnel leading to 3-17; and, as we approached it, a sight of horror met our eyes. A wriggling, writhing mass of tissue had spread across the water from the main island of Morbus and now completely covered the little island. Hideous heads looked up at us screaming defiance; hands stretched forth futilely to clutch us.

I searched for the mouth of the tunnel; but it was not visible, being entirely covered by the writhing mass. My heart sank, for I felt certain that the mass must have entered the tunnel and found its way to 3-17; for I was sure that it would enter any opening and follow the line of least resistance until it met some impassable barrier.

However, I clung desperately to the hope that I had covered the mouth of the tunnel sufficiently well to have prevented the mass from starting down it. But even so, how could we hope to reach the tunnel through that hideous cordon of horror?

John Carter stood by the rail with several members of his staff. Janai, Ras Thavas, and I were close beside him. He was gazing down with evident horror upon Ras Thavas's creation. Presently he issued instructions to the members of his staff, and two of them left to put them into effect. Then we waited, no one speaking, silenced by the horror surging beneath us, screaming, mouthing, gesticulating.

Janai was standing close to me, and presently she grasped my arm. It was the first time that she had ever voluntarily touched me. "How horrible!" she whispered. "It cannot be possible that Vor Daj's body still exists, for that horrid mass must have spread everywhere through the buildings as well as out beyond the walls of the City.

I shook my head. I had nothing to say. She pressed my arm tightly. "Tor-dur-bar, promise me that you will do nothing rash if the body of Vor Daj is lost."

"Let's not even think of it," I said.

"But we must think of it; and you must promise me."

I shook my head. "You are asking too much," I said. "There can be no happiness for me as long as I retain the body of a hormad." I realized then that I had given myself away, but she did not seem to notice it, but just stood in silence looking down upon the awful thing beneath us.

The Ruzaar was rising now, and it continued to do so until it had gained an altitude of five or six hundred feet. Then it remained stationary again, hanging directly over that part of the little islet where the cave mouth lay. Presently an incendiary bomb fell, and the mass writhed and screamed as it burst, spreading its flaming contents in all directions.

I shall not dwell upon the horror of it, but bomb after bomb was dropped until only a mass of charred and smoking flesh lay within a radius of a hundred feet of the cave opening. Then the Ruzaar dropped closer to the ground, and I was lowered by landing tackle; and following me came Ras Thavas and two hundred warriors, the latter armed with swords and flaming torches with which they immediately attacked the mass that was already creeping back to cover the ground that it had lost.

My heart was in my mouth as I fell to work to remove the earth and stones with which I had blocked the entrance to the tunnel; but as I worked, I saw no sign that it had been pierced, and presently it lay open before me and I could

156

have shouted with joy, for the mouth of the tunnel was empty.

I cannot describe my feelings as I again traversed that long tunnel back to 3–17. Was my body still there? Was it safe and whole? I conjured all sorts of terrible things that might have happened to it during my long absence. I almost ran through the black tunnel in my haste to learn the truth, and at last with trembling hands I raised the cover of the trap that led from the tunnel up into the chamber. A moment later, I stood in 3–17.

Lying as I had left it was the body of Vor Daj.

Ras Thavas soon joined me; and I could see that he, too, breathed a sigh of relief as he discovered the body and paraphernalia intact.

Without waiting for instructions from Ras Thavas, I stretched myself upon the ersite slab beside my own body; and presently Ras Thavas was bending over me. I felt a slight incision and a little pain, and then consciousness left me.

CHAPTER XXXI

ADVENTURE'S END

I OPENED MY EYES. Ras Thavas was leaning over me. Beside me lay the body of the hormad, Tor-dur-bar. I know that then the tears came to my eyes, tears of such relief and happiness and joy as I had never experienced before in my life, not so much because I had regained my own body but because now I might lay it at the feet of Janai.

"Come, my son," said Ras Thavas. "We have been here a long time. The mass is writhing and screaming in the corridor beyond the door. Let us hope that it has not succeeded in recovering the ground that it lost at the other end of the tunnel."

"Very well," I said, "let us return at once." I stepped from the table and stood again erect upon my own feet. I was just a little stiff, and Ras Thavas noticed it.

"That will pass in a moment," he said. "You have been dead a long time." And he smiled.

I stood for a moment looking down upon the uncouth body of Tor-dur-bar. "It served you well," said Ras Thavas.

"Yes," I assented, "and the best reward that I can offer it is eternal oblivion. We shall leave it here, buried forever in the pits beneath the building where it first felt life. I leave it, Ras Thavas, without a pang of regret."

"It had great strength, and, from what I understand, a good sword arm," commented the Master Mind of Mars.

"Yet I still think that I can endure life without it," I said.

"Vanity, vanity!" exclaimed Ras Thavas. "You, a warrior, would give up enormous strength and an incomparable sword arm for a handsome face."

I saw that he was laughing at me; but the whole world might laugh if it wished, just as long as I had my own body back again.

We hastened back through the tunnel, and when we finally emerged onto the islet again, warriors were still fighting back the insistent growth. Four times the detachment had been relieved since we had descended from the Ruzaar. It had been early morning when we arrived, and now the sun was just about to dip below the far horizon, yet to me it seemed but the matter of a few moments since I had descended from the Ruzaar.

We were quickly hoisted aboard again where we were fairly smothered with congratulations.

John Carter placed a hand upon my shoulder. "I could not have been more concerned over the fate of a son of mine than I have been over yours," he said.

That was all that he said, but it meant more to me than volumes spoken by another. Presently he noted my eyes wandering about the deck, and a smile touched his lips. "Where is she?" I asked.

"She could not stand the strain of waiting," he said, "and she has gone to her cabin to lie down. You had better go and tell her yourself."

"Thank you, sir," I said; and a few moments later I was knocking at the door of Janai's cabin.

"Who knocks?" she asked.

"Vor Daj," I replied, and then without waiting for an invitation I pushed open the door and entered.

She rose and came toward me, her eyes wide with questioning. "It is really you?" she asked.

"It is I," I assured her, and I crossed toward her. I wanted to take her in my arms and tell her that I loved her; but she seemed to anticipate what I had in mind, for she stopped me with a gesture.

"Wait," she said. "Do you realize that I scarcely know Vor Daj?"

I had not thought of that, but it was true. She knew Tor-dur-bar far better. "Answer me one question."

"What is it?" I asked.

"How did Teeaytan-ov die?" she demanded.

It was a strange question. What had that to do with Janai or with me? "Why, he died in the corridor leading to 3–17, struck down by one of the hormad warriors while we were escaping from the Laboratory Building," I replied.

Her white teeth flashed in a sudden smile. "Now what were you going to say to me when I stopped you?"

"I was going to tell you that I loved you," I replied, "and ask you if there was any hope that you might return my love."

"I scarcely knew Vor Daj," she said; "it was Tor-dur-bar that I learned to love; but now I know the truth that for some time I have guessed, and I realize the sacrifice that you were willing to make for me." She came and put her dear arms about my neck, and for the first time I felt the lips of the woman I loved on mine.

* * * * *

For ten days the great fleet cruised high above Morbus, dropping bombs upon the city and the island and the great mass that had started to spread out in all directions to engulf a world; nor would John Carter leave until the last vestige of the horror had been entirely exterminated. At last the bows of the great battleships were turned toward Helium; and with only a brief stop at Phundahl to return Pandar to his native city we cruised on toward home, and for Janai and me, a happiness that we had passed together through horrors to achieve.

As the great towers of the twin cities appeared in the distance, Janai and I were standing together in the bow of the Ruzaar. "I wish you would tell me," I said, "why you asked me that time how Teeaytan-ov died. You knew as well as I."

"Stupid!" she exclaimed, laughing. "Tor-dur-bar, Pandar, and I were the only survivors of that fight who were with the fleet when we returned to Morbus. Of these three, you could have seen only Tor-dur-bar before you saw me. Therefore, when you answered me correctly, I knew that Tor-dur-bar's brain had been transferred to your skull. That was all that I wanted to know, for it was the brain that gave the character and fineness to Tor-dur-bar that I had learned to love; and I do not care, Vor Daj, whose brain it was originally.

159

If you do not care to tell me, I shall never ask; but I suspect that it was your own and that you had it transferred to the head of Tor-dur-bar so that you might better protect me from Ay-mad."

"It is my own brain," I said.

"Was, you mean," she laughed; "it is mine now."